Smith's
MONTHLY

Every Month Original
Novels, Stories, and Articles

USA Today Bestselling Writer
Dean Wesley Smith

TABLE OF CONTENTS

Smith's Monthly Issue #31

Introduction
A NEW SERIES

I didn't mean to start a new series. Honest, I didn't.

But last July, when I wrote 32 short stories in 31 days, I wrote two stories about an assassin by the name of Mary Jo.

When my wonderful wife, writer and editor Kristine Kathryn Rusch, read the two stories, she said they would make a good new series.

I think I shuddered.

Honest. I shuddered.

Why?

Because I have a bunch of series going on right now.

Not a bunch, a whole bunch, a large amount, more than I can remember.

You get the idea.

Let me see if I can list some of the series I have going on.

- Thunder Mountain, a time travel series usually set in the Old West of Idaho and Oregon.

- Seeders Universe, an epic space opera series that spans galaxies.

- Poker Boy, a series following the adventures of a superhero in the gambling universe.

- Bryant Street, a series of short stories about the fear of subdivisions and mundane life.

- Ghost of a Chance, a series of novels and short stories about ghosts who save the world.

- Cold Poker Gang, a series about retired detectives who solve cold cases in Las Vegas.

- Doc Hill Thrillers, a series following a professional poker player and his team as they solve crimes.

- Buffalo Jimmy, a series (with only one book so far) following a young man and his friends through the Old West.

- Earth Protection League, an sf series of stories and one novel that follow old people taken from nursing homes to save the galaxy.

- Pilgrim Hugh Incident, a series with a very rich detective who rides around

---

Thanks for the Support

Dean Wesley Smith

in a limo and solves very strange cases very quickly.

- Golf Thrillers, a series where two Seattle detectives travel to play golf and end up solving crimes.
- Buckey the Space Pirate, a series of short stories with a guy who dresses in costumes talking with an oak tree that does limericks.

I have a hunch I have forgotten some.

And now, with this volume I add in one more series to that list:

Mary Jo Assassin, a series following an ancient and deadly assassin working and living in modern America.

If you have been following and reading all thirty issues of this magazine before this one, you are familiar with the series, and more than likely have favorites.

In this volume, I have also included a Poker Boy story, a Pilgrim Hugh story, a Cold Poker Gang story that kicked off another novel, and a Bryant Street story.

I hope Mary Jo becomes a favorite after this issue. I do plan on writing more stories in her world. After all, following an assassin can be a lot of fun.

Just don't try to outsmart her.

Thanks for reading.

—Dean Wesley Smith
Lincoln City, Oregon
April 15th, 2016

Coming Next Issue in *Smith's Monthly*
THEY'RE BACK!
A Poker Boy Short Novel

Poker Boy often solves problems and saves the world with his mutant talent of asking stupid questions.

Sometimes really stupid questions.

So when he asks the seemingly simple question over lunch one day about how the gods originated, he stirs up more than even Poker Boy bargains for.

So how did the gods originate way back before Atlantis? Might be better to just not ask. Too late for Poker Boy. He asked.

GODS HAVE HISTORY
A Poker Boy Story

ONE

I HAD LEARNED a long time ago for me, meaning about five years or so, that there was no such thing as perfect answers.

Every answer I seemed to get over the years to my often-stupid questions seemed to have more than one answer. Or worse yet, the answer was shaded in "it depends" which is a color that seems to be more like a cloud of mist.

Today, the question I had asked of Patty and Stan seemed to be getting a combination of "it depends" and more than one answer.

A double whammy.

Patty Ledgerwood, aka Front Desk Girl worked as a superhero in the hotel and lodging part of the world. Stan, my direct boss, was the God of Poker. As Poker Boy, a superhero, I worked for him and made my living playing poker when not running around saving people or the entire planet.

But even though Stan was my boss, basically I ran the team and he was part of the team. It was a complicated relationship, but we both seemed to be just fine with it. I knew he was the boss, he understood I was, at times, so new to this business of gods and superheroes, that I had no idea what was happening.

I was just good at questions that seemed to poke others into action and thus save the world from whatever evil was threatening it at the moment.

Patty and Stan and I were sitting in the big diner booth in the center of my invisible floating office over Las Vegas. Besides a few chairs, the booth was the only furniture in the big square glass room. The booth looked like I had lifted it from a 1950s diner.

The walls of my office were perfectly clear and I had put a wood railing about belt high all the way around the room so I didn't feel like I might fall off the floor at any moment.

Patty, who had her long brown hair pulled back and was wearing a wonderful white blouse and jeans instead of her normal MGM Grand front desk uniform, sat beside me. She had brown eyes that could hold me frozen it seemed and her touch actually could calm me. That was one of her many superpowers.

She had a day off and after lunch we were planning on jumping to our new home that was being built in the Oregon Coastal Range to see how things were moving along. And then we planned on having a nice dinner in Portland at a restaurant we both loved there before jumping back here for a movie and other activities that often happened on date night.

Stan had on a button-down gray sweater, gray slacks, and loafers. His hair was cut short and he was the most forgettable-looking person I had ever met. He took the "not be noticed" approach to poker while I had always taken the more flamboyant approach by wearing a black fedora-like hat and a black leather coat all the time.

Can't Get Enough of Poker Boy?
These stories and more are available at your favorite booksellers.

I considered that coat and hat my superhero costume. Not sure if it actually helped me, but it sure felt like it did at times. And besides, I liked it.

The question I had asked had been simple, or so I thought. "When did the gods actually start. And how?"

I was really tired of always being surprised by my lack of knowledge of the thousands of gods and more thousands of other superheroes that roamed the planet taking care of every tiny niche of human life. In fact, right now we were waiting for milkshakes and burgers to be brought to us by Madge, who owned a real diner in downtown Vegas where my team used to meet before we got this office. Madge was a superhero in the food service area.

Also, it seemed that at five years, I was one of the youngest of all superheroes working. I had been an orphan growing up, so I had no idea who birthed a superhero kid. Not a clue.

Superheroes basically stopped aging in their late twenties and could live forever, from what I understand. I had no idea how old exactly Patty was, but I know it was hundreds and hundreds of years older than me.

I would like to say that being in love with an older woman didn't bother me, and most of the time it didn't. But every so often she would reveal a part of her past from hundreds of years earlier and I would feel pretty darned inadequate.

I usually got over it quickly when she kissed me. More than likely another one of her superpowers. I didn't mind at all.

So my question about the origin of the gods had been with the idea that Patty and Stan could help me start to fill in some knowledge gaps.

But Stan had just laughed and said, "Not really sure, to be honest."

Stan was a master at avoiding a direct answer and that felt like a real avoidance. I knew Stan had been alive in the Atlantis days. We had even rescued his two missing daughters from that time. So he had to have had some idea.

Patty had smiled at me. "Why would that matter?"

"So you know?" I asked her.

"I honestly don't," she said.

Stan shrugged.

Can't Get Enough of Poker Boy?
These stories and more are available at your favorite booksellers.

At that point, Madge came up carrying a cheeseburger basket with fries for Stan and one for me and Patty to split.

She also had a vanilla milkshake for Stan and one for me and Patty. The milkshakes were so huge and rich and wonderful that Patty and I were lucky to even get through half of one each.

Stan always managed to finish one of his own.

The cheeseburger and fries smelled wonderful and Patty grabbed the salt shaker to salt the fries.

"Madge," I said, "Do you know the origin of the gods and superheroes? About when they started and how?"

She laughed. "Do I look that old to you?"

"Don't answer that," Patty said to me, laughing.

"Just thought I would try to learn a little history today is all," I said, raising my hands in surrender.

"I honestly have no idea," Madge said, laughing, as she vanished into the portal leading back down to her diner.

Now I was really puzzled. I glanced at Stan. "Do you think Ben could join us for lunch?"

"You're not going to let this go, are you?" Stan asked, staring at me to try to get a read on me.

"Do I ever let anything go?" I asked.

Both he and Patty laughed and then he vanished.

I turned to Patty as she started to pick up her half of the cheeseburger. "You honestly don't know?"

"I don't," she said. "Honestly, until you asked the question, never thought about it."

She bit into her half of the cheeseburger as my warning bells in the back of my head started to go off.

Patty didn't know.

Stan didn't know or wouldn't say.

Madge didn't know.

I had a hunch that I had just stuck my finger into a large hornet's nest and didn't even know it.

Typical for me and my stupid questions.

Just damn typical.

TWO

STAN APPEARED ABOUT one minute later with Ben, the oldest superhero I had ever met, at least in looks.

Ben looked like a college professor, with bifocal glasses and a tweed jacket and vest that he seemed to always wear. He had been the god of lamplighters, but Stan and I had found him one day, almost faded completely away and got him to move to be a god in the books and library area. That had perked him back up and he was happy.

It seems that for centuries and centuries, he read everything he could, including the entire library of Alexandria, which was now part of the Library of Atlantis. And he remembered everything he had read.

So he had become the historian of my team, the person we turned to when information from the past might save our lives. Amazing how often it did.

"Stan tells me you are trying to learn some history," Ben said, sliding into the booth next to Stan. "As I have offered in the past, I am always willing to help."

"I appreciate that," I said, wiping my mouth of any stray ketchup from the burger. "My question seemed simple, but turns out it's not. Basically I was curious as to how the gods and superheroes started. And how we became immortal and all that."

Patty and Stan and I all watched Ben as his face went white.

Now some major alarm bells were going off in my head. I had really stumbled into it now.

Stan glanced at me, raised an eyebrow. He was surprised as well and more than likely feeling the same worry.

Damn, it had been a nice lunch and I had gone and ruined it by my stupid questions.

Ben took a deep breath and turned to Stan. "I think we need to talk with Laverne."

Now both of Stan's eyebrows went up and he nodded, put down the fry he had been about to eat and the two of them vanished.

Laverne was the most powerful god working right now. She was Lady Luck herself. The more I learned about her, the more powerful I understood she actually was.

"Got any idea what I just caused?" I asked Patty.

She just shook her head. "Maybe there's a reason I didn't know the answer to your question."

"My little voice is telling me it's not a good reason," I said.

"It's not a bad reason either," Laverne said as she and Stan and Ben appeared.

Ben and Stan slid back into the booth and Laverne pulled up a chair at the end of the booth and took one of Stan's fries.

Laverne had on a gray silk suit with a blue blouse under it. She had her long hair pulled back and tied off, making her classic beauty look stark and very powerful.

"I have put a shield around this office so that no one, and I mean no one, can hear what I am about to tell you four."

Suddenly I wished I had not taken as many bites of the cheeseburger as I had.

"Ben knows this," Laverne said, "and since I trust you three with the world's life at times, I figured I can trust you with this bit of history."

I nodded thanks.

"So you want to know where and how the gods and superheroes started?" Laverne asked, turning to face me.

"It seemed like a simple question," I said. "Appears it is not."

"Our official history is, of course, fairly well known," Laverne said. "We fought on the side of the elves and the dwarves to defeat the Titans, who were trying to control and dominate the world."

I nodded. "So most of the textbook stuff has truth in it?"

"It does," Laverne said. "We did not expect to be worshipped after the win and didn't much like it, to be honest, which is why we quickly went underground and our history became myths, including the god and superhero parts."

I nodded at that. That much I understood. They were all called gods, but no god I had ever met actually acted like one. They just all had powers.

"So we evolved on the planet before that?" I asked.

She shook her head. "No race that now lives on this planet originated here."

I started to open my mouth and then what she had said sunk in and I shut it.

"Even the Silicon Suckers at one point in the far distant past came here from other worlds in this galaxy," Ben said. "The Titans did as well. So did dwarves and elves, and humans and gods. The war with the Titans did not start on this planet and did not end here either."

"Is it over?" Patty asked.

"For the moment," Laverne said.

Oh, great, just great.

Stan had lost his entire poker face and was just staring at Laverne. Ben was watching Laverne, taking his lead from her, clearly.

Beside me, Patty was breathing in a slow, shallow fashion, clearly upset.

"So we are all aliens?" I asked.

"Not after forty thousand years here on the planet," Laverne said, laughing. "I think we can all be called locals just fine. Just as the Silicon Suckers and the dwarves and elves are."

"Oh," was all I could think to say.

And honestly, that felt intelligent to me at that moment.

THREE

LAVERNE LOOKED AT all four of us and smiled. "Hard to imagine, isn't it?"

"Very," Patty said.

Imagining was the least of my issues at the moment. I just wanted to get my brain working to even have a thought that made sense.

"There is something I need to show you all," Laverne said.

A moment later I found myself standing next to Patty in a dark space that smelled faintly of cleaner.

The lights came up slowly until the massive space was bright with light. What was around me made no sense at all to my poor poker brain. There were a good fifty chairs at what looked to be some sort of futuristic computer station.

All the stations were coming to life as well, showing readings in a language that looked like something from Egypt to me.

The gigantic room had a high, domed ceiling and was layered in half circles all facing a massive front wall that was blank. Most of the panels and chairs were around the walls on the top half circle.

There was a secondary circle of stations on a slightly lower level and then down in the center was a station with four chairs. Two big ones sort of melded together and one on each side of the big one.

Everything seemed to be focused on the massive blank wall that filled a third of the room in front of the lower level.

It looked like a control room for a massive power station or something.

"This is the bridge of our ship, *Olympus*," Laverne said.

Ship! What kind of ship?

Again my poor brain was going back into lockdown. For being a hero who had helped save the world a bunch of times, I was sure having trouble today just keeping it together.

"Welcome back," Chairman," a soft, female computer voice said. "Welcome Commander."

The huge screen in front of the massive room came alive, but it showed nothing but a faint light.

"It is good to be back," Laverne said.

"Agreed," Ben said.

Laverne was called Chairman and Ben had been a commander. Confused didn't even begin to describe how I was feeling. Numb seemed to be closer to accurate.

"Status of *Olympus?*" Laverne asked.

"All systems are active and on standby," the computer voice said. "All are tested regularly and any issues repaired."

"Good," Laverne said.

"Any crew on board at this point?" Ben asked.

"None of the crew has returned in over seven hundred years planet time," the ship said.

Laverne nodded. "Please recognize these three new arrivals as official members of the crew."

"Understood," the big ship said. "Welcome."

I think my brain got my body to say "Thank you."

Patty did the same.

Stan just nodded.

"*Olympus,*" Laverne said, "Can you give us an image of space outside this ship on the big screen please, aimed sunward?"

So we were on a spaceship? In space.

Good to know.

It sure didn't feel like I thought space would feel.

A massive image of stars spread out over the screen. Beautiful didn't begin to describe it. Millions and millions of stars filled that screen.

"Oh, my," Patty said.

"Please indicate the sun we orbit," Laverne said.

A line was drawn around one tiny star that looked only slightly brighter than the others. Wow, we were a long, long way out in space if that was the sun.

Laverne turned to the three of us. "We are in an orbit just outside the system where Earth lives. The ship is hidden among debris here and made to look like a small moon on the outside. It is completely shielded.

"Why?" Patty asked a half second before I could. "If you have this ship here, why didn't you just move on? Or go home. Or whatever?"

"Our home has always been *Olympus,*" Laverne said, a touch of pride in her voice. "This ship is about the same size as the

Earth moon and can hold hundreds of thousands at any given point."

"Were you born on this ship?" I asked Laverne.

She shook her head. "I was born in a distant galaxy and recruited with my husband to have the honor to be the Chairman of this wonderful ship. *Olympus* was my home for sixty thousand years before we arrived here through a series of accidents."

"So *Olympus* is working?" I asked.

"I am working, Poker Boy," the ship's voice said.

"We chose to stay and live on the planet," Ben said. "At least for a time."

A time? I had a hunch that forty thousand years was more than the time they had planned to start.

"Why?" I asked.

"Because we found aliens," Laverne said. "Three different races, actually, all growing and expanding in the same galaxy. Titans, Elves and Dwarves, and Silicon Suckers."

"Normally," Ben said, "it was rare to find even one alien race in the billions of worlds in a galaxy. We did not mingle with alien races in any way. We just gave the galaxy a wide pass and moved on. The universe is a very empty place out there. Alien races are very rare and seldom survive, let alone move between stars as the three in this galaxy have done."

"But this one planet and a dozen others, through complete error and circumstance, we had already seeded with humans in this galaxy," Laverne said. "Some of our seeder ships got out ahead of us and this galaxy was not well scouted, clearly."

"Seeder ships?" Patty asked, again a second before my brain could ask the same question.

"That was the *Olympus* mission," Laverne said. "To seed human cultures through the different galaxies."

"So once we discovered the mistake, we decided to stop," Ben said, "pull in all our ships, and go into hiding here and help the planets with humans survive."

"And thanks to this team," Laverne said, indicating me and Patty and Stan, "We are continuing to do that on the last human planet left in this galaxy."

"What happened to the others?" Stan asked.

"We lost many battles in the war," Laverne said.

There was no chance in hell I was going to ask more about that.

"Do you see a time when many of you will return to *Olympus* and move on?" Patty asked.

Laverne nodded. "At some point, in the distant future, we hope to do just that. And with many new crew members."

Laverne looked at the three of us. "But first we need to keep this planet, this last human world in this galaxy, safe for as long as we can."

That much I understood.

Saving the world made sense to me. Spaceships on the other hand were another matter altogether.

Laverne turned. "*Olympus*, would you please ask my husband to join me. We need to check in with Chairman Wade if it has been seven hundred years."

"I will be glad to, Chairman," *Olympus* said.

Laverne turned to me. "Now, we have answered the question as to our origin. But you three will need to keep it to yourselves. Most of the new gods and superheroes do not know of *Olympus* yet."

I nodded, completely understanding. "May we visit *Olympus* again to get a tour, if that would be all right with *Olympus?*"

"Yes, please," Patty said.

Stan nodded.

"I would be honored," *Olympus* said. "If the Chairman gives permission."

"They will always have my permission," Laverne said.

I nodded to Laverne. "Thank you for being honest with us."

She nodded and a moment later I was sitting next to Patty in the booth in my floating office over Las Vegas.

My half-eaten part of our cheeseburger still actually looked good.

Ben was smiling, staring at all of us.

Stan just shook his head and dug into his remaining fries and cheeseburger. I hoped someday to be that calm and collected about world-shattering news as Stan was.

"Thank you," I said to Ben.

"For exactly what?" he asked, smiling.

"For answering what seemed to be a silly question with respect."

"Our history should always be respected," he said. "Here and on *Olympus*."

"There is a lot to learn," I said.

"We have time," Ben said, smiling.

I nodded and went back to working on my cheeseburger. Before today I had thought the history here on Earth of the gods and superheroes was complex and a lot to learn. Now I also had thousands of years of *Olympus* history as well to try to figure out.

I was going to need a lot of years.

More than I could probably imagine at the moment.

A whole lot more.

~

Now Available
from all your favorite booksellers in trade paper and electronic editions.

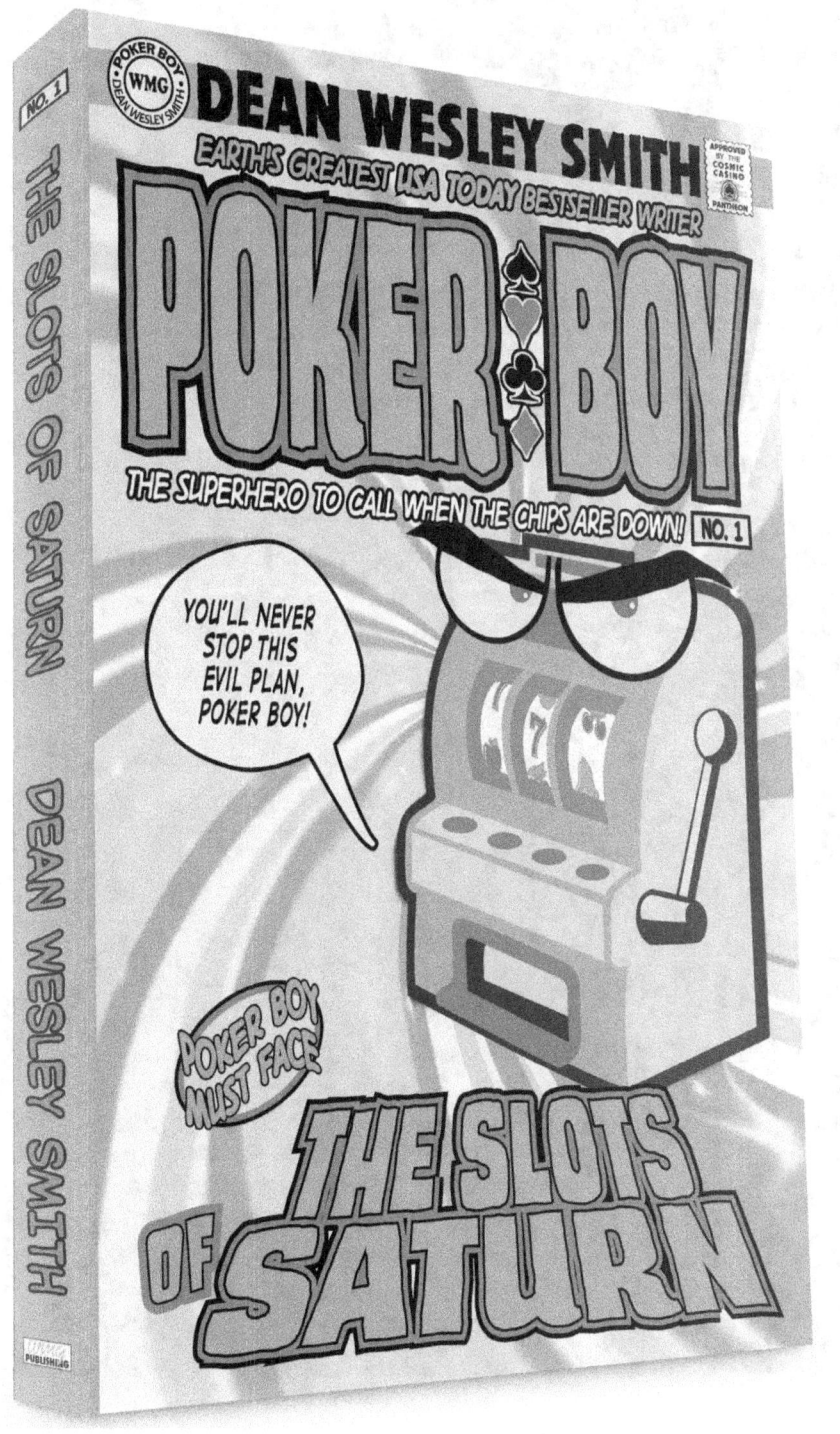

USA *Today* Bestselling Writer

DEAN WESLEY SMITH

A LONG WAY DOWN

A Bryant Street Story

Lacey Temlin hated her husband. She called him Dead Man. He cheated on her, she watched.

Her plan to kill him seemed perfect.

Lacey needed everything to always be perfect.

Until it became clear they lived in the twisted world of Bryant Street.

A LONG WAY DOWN
A Bryant Street Story

NUDE, STANDING IN the center of her kitchen, Lacey Temlin let the lukewarm and slightly bitter taste of her morning coffee settle her nerves. She drank it black, no cream or sugar to mar the desired taste. But now the coffee had sat too long after she had made it. It was the only thing not perfect around her at the moment.

Her modern, light granite kitchen counters shone with a polish she doubted they had when installed. The dark tile floors were like a mirror and every handle on the cabinets had been wiped down at least four times.

Every dish in each cabinet had been washed and put back carefully in perfect order after she had wiped down the insides of each cabinet.

The modern steel appliances didn't have a fingerprint on them and a person could eat out of the sink it was so clean.

The kitchen smelled like a combination of lemon juice and bleach. She had a hunch the smell was far stronger than she was noticing, considering how many hours she had been using the cleaner.

She eased her shoulders up and down a few times to loosen them and took another sip of her almost-cold coffee. She had made the coffee after her shower, then had spent too long in the bathroom working on her brown hair trying to get it perfect. But after three hours of intense cleaning, she had to get herself clean as well.

And perfect.

Everything had to be perfect.

And now, finally, it was.

She turned slowly in the kitchen, studying to see if she had missed any detail at all. She had even climbed up and cleaned off the top of the refrigerator. Any blood drops would be easy to find now.

She let out a deep sigh that seemed to echo in the large, suburban home. She had so loved this house when she and Dead Man had bought it. They had been so happy.

Three bedrooms that they talked about using for future children, a two-car garage where her Mercedes lived beside his Lexus, and a kitchen she always described to friends as perfect.

They had even had the back lawn that looked out over the city below refurbished and put in two swings. She had spent many a summer's night sitting in that swing staring out at the city.

She had someday hoped her children would use the swings. Now that would never happen.

And last night, she had once again sat in the swing after she discovered his affair.

She had actually walked in on Dead Man and his secretary having sex on his desk in his office after hours. His desk stuff and some papers had scattered everywhere on the floor, making an awful mess, and Dead Man and his secretary had both been so preoccupied, they didn't notice Lacey peeking in and then filming them for a minute with her phone.

The secretary had blonde hair, much larger breasts than Lacey, and a slight roll of fat around her stomach. How could Dead Man even be interested in such a woman when he had a perfect-bodied wife at home?

Lacey had no idea what had gone wrong with Dead Man's thinking.

She and Dead Man were both thirty, both successful in real estate, both in love with each other.

Clearly not enough.

The sex had slowly faded to nothing over the last two years, even though she was going to the gym every day to keep fit and trim just for him.

Yesterday, she knew that their ideal marriage in their perfect home was over. Dead Man was sleeping with his secretary and there was no returning to marriage bliss from that.

In fact, in short order, there would be no more marriage. Period.

Perfect had been ruined for good for her.

She knew she could never live without perfect in her life. Perfect had become everything she lived for, actually.

And there was no point in continuing to live without perfect.

She took the half-cup of cold coffee and went down the tiled hall and into their master bedroom. The bed was made exactly, everything in its exact place on the dresser and vanity. She had laid out on the bed the perfect dress for the evening, something with some lace and trim and a nice pattern. Not a going-out-to-dinner dress, but not her exercise clothes either.

When she bought it, Dead Man had said it made her look younger and sexier.

She put it on, not bothering with underwear. The dress would be ruined anyway, so there was no point in also destroying perfectly fine underwear as well.

She then took her coffee cup, still half-full, and went back into their living room. On the inlaid mahogany coffee table in front of the big screen television, she had set up her phone to play Dead Man's sex scene with his secretary over and over again.

Luckily she hadn't recorded the sound of the sex. She would never want to hear that again.

She put her coffee cup on the table beside her phone, adjusting it so it looked like she had placed it there naturally. Then she did the unthinkable just a day ago.

She tipped it over, letting the coffee run away from her phone and off the coffee table and onto the tile floor.

At first she wanted to jump up and grab a cloth and clean up the mess. Then she realized that the mess was exactly what she wanted, what she had planned, and she forced herself to calm down.

Perfect.

She had made a perfect mess.

She glanced at the time on the big decorative wall clock over the kitchen.

Any moment now. Dead Man was always punctual coming home at exactly the time he said he would.

And right on time, the sound of the garage door opening rumbled faintly through the house.

She tapped the phone without shutting off the video. She had set the phone to send the film on the screen to Dead Man's boss and his secretary's husband and the police.

The message with the video to the police said simply, "He's going to kill me. I discovered his affair. Hurry."

And then she had typed in most of the Bryant Street address, but cut off the last few letters to make it seem she had been interrupted. They would find the house easily.

She sat back on the couch, staring ahead at the screen as if she was in shock. She might have been in shock when she saw the scene in his office the first time, but now it just looked disgusting and messy and actually kind of boring.

And she could actually look at it now without seeing large clawed monsters crawling on both of them.

"Lacey," Dead Man said, the way he always did when he came home and her car was in the garage, "I'm home."

That had been funny for the first few months. After that it had just grown tiring.

She could hear him come into the living room behind her and then stop.

"Did you clean up your office or did you make her?" Lacey asked.

Dead Man said nothing.

Lacey could feel the thick tension in the air and she kind of liked that. It made her feel alive for the first time in a very long time. Too bad she was about to die.

In the distance she could hear the faint sounds of sirens, more than likely the police coming.

She stood and without looking at Dead Man, walked into her perfectly cleaned kitchen.

She took a long, very sharp carving knife from the knife block on the counter, then turned and said to him, "Might as well cut my heart out."

"Wouldn't that make a mess?" he asked, turning and moving toward her.

"Yeah, it would."

"You hate messes."

"I hate you more," she said, her voice calm even though she was having trouble breathing.

"Did you get off standing in the door watching me and Darla?" Dead Man asked. "Or were we covered in monsters?"

She wanted to take the knife and stab him at that moment. It had been slightly exciting, but she would never admit that to him.

She handed him the knife. "Go ahead, make a mess."

He did exactly as she knew he would do. He took the knife by the handle and then tossed it on the counter. He didn't put it back where it belonged, he didn't put it beside the sink to be cleaned later. He just tossed it aside.

What had she ever seen in this man?

"Being a little dramatic here, aren't you?" Dead Man asked.

She smiled as the sirens outside got louder. "You ruined my life."

"I think you did that all on your own," Dead Man said, shaking his head and looking sad. "When you had that affair with the broker and brought home crabs."

She shuddered. She had forgotten that.

She had never felt clean again after that.

Everything had changed.

Every time she and Dead Man had tried to make love after that, she imagined giant creatures swarming all over him. Twice she had thrown up on him.

And professional help had done no good.

In fact, it was the professionals who suggested that to get past the mistake she had made and the problems she had caused and the images of giant crab-like monsters on people and herself, she needed to keep clean.

Now she kept everything clean.

"So you called the police again?" Dead Man said, shaking his head and looking at her.

She could no longer tell what his expressions meant.

"Again?" she asked, feeling confused.

Dead Man pointed to the screen in the living room replaying his affair. "Lacey, you know, if you let yourself remember, that's not me. That's an old clip you found on the Internet five months ago. You just believe it's me and my secretary to make yourself feel better."

Three Cold Poker Gang Novels
Available at your favorite booksellers.

She glanced at the screen of the man going at the woman on the desk. Of course that was Dead Man. She had watched him, she had caught him, she had filmed him.

"You want me to have an affair so that everything is even. You said that once. But I only love you. Only you."

Her perfect plan was falling apart.

"As the doctors told you," Dead Man said, "you are just trying to blame me for your affair."

"You ruined our perfect life," she said, trying to keep her voice level, but she knew she couldn't hold on much more.

"I have never had an affair," he said. "You had the affair and ruined our perfect life. You are the one that can't seem to let go of the fact that you caught crabs and let us move on together. I have forgiven you from day one. Remember? You need to forgive yourself."

She shook her head violently from side-to-side.

"That's not true!"

"Of course it's true, Lacey," Dead Man said.

Behind them the police knocked and then came in. One was a young man looking puzzled and the other was an older guy by the name of Donny. She knew him from somewhere.

"Lacey having troubles again?" Donny asked, looking genuinely concerned as he came up and stood beside Dead Man.

"More than likely forgot to take her meds again," Dead Man said.

"The place does smell of cleaning solution," Donny said, nodding.

Lacey couldn't believe all this was happening. They were talking about her as if she wasn't there. Her perfect plan was ruined. They had got to her before she could stab herself and make it look like Dead Man did it.

"I'm sorry, Devin," Donny said. "What can we do?"

"Just leave me alone!" Lacey shouted.

She bolted for the back door and out into the yard. There she climbed into the swing that looked out over the beautiful lights of the city. The stars were out and there was a full moon.

She made herself take a few deep breaths and gaze out over the perfect view.

This was perfect.

Absolutely perfect.

From the porch she heard Donny say, "We have an ambulance on the way."

"Thanks," Dead Man said. "That will be perfect."

Both he and Donny chuckled slightly, but Lacey thought they were right.

Perfect.

~

USA TODAY BESTSELLING AUTHOR

DEAN WESLEY
SMITH

LAYING THE MUSIC
TO REST

A former college professor turned bartender, Doc finds himself trying to save his friends from a ghost under a lake in the wilderness of Idaho.

From diving into a ghost town buried under a lake to trying to stay alive on the sinking deck of the Titanic, this time-travel science fiction novel reads like a roller-coaster ride with all the twists and turns.

First published in paperback in 1989 from Warner Questar Books, Dean Wesley Smith's first published novel gives a lot of hints of his future series and his bestselling career spanning over a hundred and fifty novels.

Published here in its original form, without any changes, just as Dean wrote it almost thirty years ago.

LAYING THE MUSIC TO REST
Part 4

CHAPTER SIX

Monumental Lodge
June 28, 1990

I AWOKE TO Fred banging on my door and announcing breakfast. I was amazed that I hadn't had nightmares all night. But in fact, I had slept right through and felt something just short of what I am sure death feels like.

Somehow I crawled out of bed without screaming from all the stiff muscles. I felt a little better after a good, hot shower. Not much, but a little.

Fred was cooking the best-smelling bacon I could have ever imagined as I eased my sore body down the stairs. I was the last to arrive. Constance, Steven, and Susan were all sitting at the kitchen table reading newspapers.

"Morning," Constance said as I hit the bottom of the stairs and padded across the room in my bare feet. "Sleep okay?"

"Like a drunk," I said. "How about you, Fred?"

"Didn't even notice Constance's snoring."

"That's because I was awake listening to yours," she said without looking up from her paper.

"Coffee on the stove," Fred said, pointing with a fork at the pot.

I glanced at one of the newspapers as I passed the table. The date at the top was yesterday's. "Where'd you get the papers?"

"Mail drop this morning," Fred said. "Didn't you hear the plane?"

"I didn't hear a thing from the time my head hit that pillow to the time you knocked on the door. Nothing."

"Plane drops off our mail, guest arrivals, and newspapers twice a week in the clearing above the lake. If we're not there to wave at it, or have already put a red flag on one of the small trees beside the meadow, they send in the rescue squad. It's kind of our safety net in case something really bad goes wrong and neither one of us can get to help. The guy lives down in Yellow Pine and he also lets us know when guests are on their way in. He's our contact with the real world."

"Good thinking," I said. "Considering how far out in the boondocks this is."

"Oh, we're not that bad," Constance said. "There are ranches down on the Middle Fork that are a hundred miles from the nearest road."

"But don't they have airstrips?" I asked as I filled my cup and went over to the table. "Morning," I said as Susan looked up.

"Some of them," Constance said.

"Good morning," Susan said without so much as a smile. She went back to reading her paper. She was obviously still mad at me for laughing at her last night. Hell, with a story like her "I'm a time traveler from the future" one, what did she expect? I'd tried to be open-minded. I'd listened as long as I could keep a straight face. If I hadn't been so tired, I might have lasted longer.

I studied her for a moment. She looked tired. Last night, after our "talk," I hadn't told anyone about her strange rantings. I had been too damn pooped to fight it through. Fred had asked me what went on and I had told him I'd give him a good laugh in the morning. I had mentioned keeping the mirror with me, but he suggested a safer place under a floorboard in their bedroom. So that's where we had put it. I noticed that it was now back sitting on the fireplace. I also noticed that Susan's pack was leaning against the wall.

Somewhere in the middle of my shower, I had decided that we should let Susan play with the mirror before I told Fred and Constance her story. It made more sense that way. Let her prove herself nuts without me doing or saying a thing. Maybe then we could get on to something that might help.

Nothing was mentioned about the mirror until after everyone was finished reading the paper and stuffing themselves on Fred's incredibly good bacon, eggs, and home-baked bread. I swore three times I couldn't eat another bite and then found myself, because of the smell of the bread or the taste of the bacon, taking more.

Somehow, I finally pulled myself away from the table and motioned for Fred that he should join me out on the front porch as I staggered for the front door.

The sun wasn't yet above the mountain, leaving the porch buried in shadows and a sharp, cold bite in the air. It felt refreshing. I did a few quick stretches to try to loosen a dozen more sore muscles, then went over to the log rail and leaned on it. This morning the water looked blue-gray. My imagination still could not grasp the fact that there used to be a town sitting there. It was too much a picture postcard lake to have such a strange history.

Behind me, Fred pulled the front door closed. "Great breakfast," I said. I tapped my stomach. If I survived this trip, I was going to be doing sit-ups for a month.

"Thanks," he said. "You find out any more about our guest last night? I noticed you two were being a little cold to each other over breakfast. She turn your pass down?"

"Didn't even give it a try. You know I like redheads. This one is too weird to make an exception."

"That bad, huh? I have an uneasy feeling about her myself."

"Totally crazy doesn't come close. She now claims she's from the future. Or something like that. It all sounded more like the ravings of an asylum escapee. I don't know what to make of it."

"You have got to be kidding." Fred's eyes were wide.

I shook my head. "Nope. She was dead serious. And she wants to try a few things with the mirror."

Fred shook his head. "Not a chance this side of hell. Let's get her on a horse and headed back up that trail."

"Hang on. I was figuring we should let her play with it for a few minutes. Let her play out her fantasy and then send her packing."

Fred laughed. "That does make more sense. But we can't let her hurt it."

"I doubt she would. She seems to think it's incredibly important."

"Hell, what more did she say? The bacon in my stomach is twisting with curiosity."

I laughed. "Do me a favor and let me wait a little longer. I think you'll end up with most of it as she plays with the mirror. Besides, if you and Constance are asking her questions we can twist her up in no time. No one could keep a story like hers straight for long. It was too off the wall."

Fred nodded. "So we let her do what she wants with the mirror, within reason. We'll both stay close to her, in case. She's crazy enough to try anything."

"You called it," I said.

I took one more quick look down at the lake and then held the door open for Fred as we went back inside.

***

I told Susan that we had decided she was free to try her experiments, as long as she didn't damage the mirror. I took the mirror off the mantel and laid it glass up on the coffee table. Then I sat down on the couch beside the table so that I could easily reach the mirror.

"Thanks," she said, and nodded at me as she leaned the pack against the over-stuffed chair and sat down.

Fred came over and stood in front of the fireplace with its small daytime fire. When I looked up, he nodded at me and then at the rifle leaning beside the fireplace behind him. He was ready for anything. Smart man.

Constance and Steven sat down on the other couch.

"Exactly what is it you're trying to do?" Fred asked.

Susan glanced at me.

"I haven't told them a thing," I said, and then smiled. She didn't look happy.

She picked up the mirror, studied it for a moment, and then glanced up at

Fred. "I'm trying to trigger this device and go where the ghost's lover went."

"And where might that be?" Fred asked. Fred was playing it a lot straighter than I could. He wasn't even smiling.

Susan shrugged. "I'm not really sure. Any one of two dozen or so places." Carefully, she rubbed her hand along the back of the mirror, then looked into the glass and laid the mirror on the table.

We all waited in silence.

Nothing.

"Damn," she said. "There has to be some sequence of events that wouldn't often occur naturally, but would occur with enough frequency to pull the required number of people."

"You know where these places are?" I asked.

Susan nodded. "Of course."

"Then why don't you go directly there, instead of through the mirror? Would seem to make more sense."

"We can't. All the original locations are shielded from us. The only way in is through the original devices."

"Are they all mirrors?"

"No," she said. "But they are all glass of some sort or another. It's the special glass that with a boost of power warps time and allows passage through it."

"So you mean to say this mirror is a machine of some sort?" Constance asked. "I don't see how that can be. It's too small."

"Not really a machine. More like what the doctor said earlier. A focus. In very crude terms, the glass works like a magnifying glass works on the sun's rays. This glass focuses spatiotemporal currents, time waves if you will. Somehow, with the right sequence of events, a burst of power from a source location is triggered and pulls the person who triggers

it through the glass and to the source. It's the same principle that our return devices work on. Only hidden."

"Your return what?" Fred asked.

Again Susan looked over at me, then back up at Fred. "My people use something similar." She took the mirror and rubbed the handle a few times, then looked into it and again laid it face up on the table.

We waited. I noticed that Susan seemed to be holding her breath.

Again, nothing happened.

"Maybe Gretchen turned down the marriage proposal," Constance said. "Try turning it facedown."

Both Fred and I gave Constance a hard look and she shrugged.

Susan nodded and started to again pick up the mirror. But as she reached for it, the air in front of the coffee table shimmered and the ghost appeared. She spooked me almost as bad as she had the day before. Only this time I kept my seat on the couch near the mirror. As she firmed up, the room temperature dropped twenty degrees. I could see why all the lodge guests had left.

I glanced over at Steven as Fred made a hasty retreat around the back of the couch and away from the ghost. Steven again had that glassy-eyed look and was slumped back against the couch, staring off at the ceiling.

The ghost stood and looked at the mirror for a moment, as if checking to make sure it was all right. Then she faded out and was gone.

Constance rushed over to Steven as he slowly shook his head. I felt sorry for him. It was bad enough having that ghost pop in and out, but being able to sense her, read her thoughts, must have been awful. I was glad it was him instead of me.

Susan stared at Steven. "Did you get anything more from her?"

Steven nodded. "Constance was right," he said, his voice again very weak. "Alex put his image in the mirror, then gave it to Gretchen. She turned the mirror facedown."

"Was there anything else?" Susan asked. "*Just* before he looked into the mirror?"

"No," Steven said after a short pause. "I have this picture of him simply wiping the mirror off, looking into it, and handing it to Gretchen. She turned him down and that was when he left. She wants him to return."

Steven's answer seemed to have satisfied Susan. She held the mirror up in front of her and rubbed the frame along the right side as she kept her image in it. Then she turned it facedown.

And waited. Nothing.

She picked the mirror back up and tried rubbing the left side.

Nothing.

On the third try she found what she was looking for. She held the mirror up in front of her and ran her hand completely around the frame. As if she were cleaning it with a rag, she started at the handle and went clockwise around and back to the handle.

Then she laid the mirror facedown on the table.

Suddenly, she smiled, grabbed her pack, and pulled it up in her lap.

I grabbed the mirror, pulling it out of her reach. She seemed to think she was going somewhere and I didn't want her taking the mirror with her.

She didn't. She saw my action and smiled at me. She faded, shimmering as if we were looking at her through heat waves coming off hot desert sand.

"Thanks," she said to me, nodding at the mirror. "Keep it safe. Others will want to use it very soon." Her voice sounded as if she had shouted it down a long tunnel and the look in her eyes was one of success. An ugly look that chilled me almost as much as the ghost had.

She faded and I could see the chair through her.

Then she was gone.

You could have cut the silence and tension in that room with a dull knife.

"Holy shit," Fred said softly.

I laid the mirror back down on the coffee table, being very careful to make sure it was facing up. Then I stood on what felt like rubber legs and headed for Fred's liquor cabinet. If there was ever a reason to have a drink before lunch, this was it.

I wasn't going to let the opportunity slip by.

CHAPTER SEVEN

Monumental Cemetery
June 28, 1990

ALL PEOPLE IN the world, unless they go through life doing absolutely nothing, and I have known just such people, have a few moments in their lives when their world changes direction. For most, the shifts are gradual, like a slow curve on an interstate highway. The change of direction isn't really noted unless in hindsight. "Oh, hey. Isn't it amazing that I was going to be a heart surgeon and now I'm selling real estate?" People like that never really know the exact time the change took place. It just did.

But changes in my life have been along the line of running into a brick wall. I've run into a number of small brick walls in my life. But only two major ones. The first was the exact moment Fred told me Carla was dead. Killed in a stupid car accident. I knew without a doubt that at that moment, my life had completely changed. And it had.

The second time was today. When I laid that mirror back on that table and headed for the bar, I knew without a doubt that my life would never be the same. That the easy, don't feel-or-do-anything way of life of the last few years at the Garden Lounge had suddenly ended.

I flopped down on the couch after I had made myself a drink, downed it, made one each for Steven, Constance, and Fred, then made myself a second. Where the hell had Susan gone? I stared at the empty chair and then at the mirror. Was she in the same place as Alex, a man who had supposedly disappeared eighty years earlier? Where the hell would that be? In 1990, there were very few places in the world that could hide a large number of people for eighty years. Let alone a few dozen such places.

Fred dropped onto the other couch and stared at the mirror. "Maybe you should tell us what she said last night."

"You know, I didn't believe one word she said. I do now and I'm scared to death."

"That bad, huh?" Fred asked.

I nodded and motioned for Constance and Steven to sit down. This was going to take a while.

Susan's chair was left open, as if she might appear at any moment. It took about thirty minutes to relay what Susan had told me the night before. Now

I wished I had asked more questions, because damned if I could answer half of the ones the three of them threw at me. I just hadn't believed her, so I hadn't bothered. Instead I had laughed.

But I told them what I could remember of her story about how she was from the near future and how all of the people then were descendants of what she called seed groups, people taken randomly from our culture. She had said there were four such main groups. When I had asked her why she had been trying to find the mirror, she'd tried to explain a little about how her world was in conflict, with both sides trying to find the original groups of the other.

When I had managed to ask her what had happened to our present world, she wouldn't say. But she made it very clear that during her time, there were only the seed groups left.

"Pretty farfetched," Fred said after I was finished with the part of her story about how one of the groups called Lomax was a genetically altered group. "What do you make of it all?"

I pointed at the empty chair. "After that, I don't know what to think. It makes sense that something like we witnessed with Susan happened to the ghost's lover. Would tend to shake anyone up, especially someone in 1909. Shook the hell out of me, and I've watched a dozen 'Beam me up, Scotties' on television."

"I agree," Fred said. "It would explain the ghost's lover disappearing."

"And it would also explain," Steven said, "why Gretchen was so traumatized into waiting around for him after she was killed."

"So how come these seed groups are fighting?" Fred asked. "And why are they looking for these mirrors?"

I shrugged. "I didn't let her get that far."

"Do you think we're going to blow ourselves up?" Constance asked, her voice low.

"I read the morning paper. Nothing major seems to be going on at the moment. But you never know. There are a lot of crazies in this world."

"And not all of them are in Russia." Fred said.

"I'll drink to that," I said, and downed half of my drink to try to clear that image from my mind.

We all sat in silence for a few minutes.

"One thing to remember," I said, breaking the silence in the big room. "We still haven't solved the problem of the ghost. And now she pops in and out of here like an unwanted in-law. Anyone got any ideas?"

"Somehow," Steven said, "Alex must return. That is the only thing I am completely convinced will free Gretchen's spirit."

"Lovely," Fred said.

"Maybe Susan will help him get back," Constance said. "If she went to the same place and wasn't lying about all that time travel stuff, she might."

"I doubt it," I said. "But I suppose there is always hope. Assuming that this Alex is still alive after all this time."

I let that sink in for a moment, then said, "I need to take a walk. How about we all do some thinking. Maybe there's something we're all missing."

No one disagreed, so I grabbed my coat and wandered down across the log-jam and up a trail under the trees growing on the old mudslide. I found it hard to imagine that at one time, this entire area had slid down and blocked the valley. I looked up through the thirty-foot-tall pine trees and then back at the smooth forest floor and just couldn't imagine it.

But it had happened, the same as the ghost had led us to the mirror and Susan had disappeared right out of a chair in the middle of the lodge. There was no getting

Thunder Mountain Short Novels
Available at your favorite booksellers.

around the reality of it all happening. Maybe I was starting to do what I had always feared most—close my mind to new ideas.

I had hated those who refused to live in the present, but instead stuck to the values of their past without thought or reason. I had prided myself on being able to be open-minded with the kids who sat in my classes and who now came into the bar. But maybe I had been kidding myself. Maybe I was as closed-minded as the next fool.

I stopped and stared through the trees at the lake. Susan had disappeared from the lodge after triggering a mirror she called a transportation focus. That was a fact. And there was a ghost waiting for her lover. That was also a fact. The next question was what to do about it. I was starting to understand how the people of Roosevelt must have felt when they tried to fight the moving wall of mud and rock I was now standing on.

I wandered away from the lake until the trail dropped down across what Fred had said was Mule Creek. The trail forked at that point, one fork going up the Mule Creek valley in the direction of the old Dewey Mine. Fred said it was a fun place to explore. I didn't feel like exploring right at the moment.

I turned and headed down the trail along Monumental Creek, away from the lake. Fred had told me that the trail ran down into the Big Creek valley and then after that into the Middle Fork of the Salmon River. I had thought I would amble a mile or so and then turn back. I didn't make it that far.

About three hundred yards past Mule Creek, in an area of the hillside that was flatter than any other, I noticed the old cemetery.

It was above the trail and fenced off with the bleached remains of a short wood fence. A few of the markers were wood planks on which most of the writing was long gone. About fifteen stone markers dotted the brush and needles under the pines. Most were tipped at odd angles. Another four or five were knocked down. In a few places, the ground had sunk into a grave.

I read a few of the old stones. Just names and dates, mostly from a few years before the flood. One stone caught my attention. It looked newer, a little whiter, as if it had only been there half the time of the others. I walked over to it and read the simple inscription on it.

Richard Haycroft
Beloved Grandfather
1867—1943

The first and only Mayor
of Roosevelt, Idaho. He
loved the town and wanted
to be buried here.

I sat down with my back against a tree near the stone marker and stared out over the narrow valley and the creek below. I knew where I wanted to be buried. Beside Carla in Boise. But now I wondered if I was going to get that chance. Damn it all to hell.

I took a deep breath of the clear mountain air and tried to organize my thoughts into some sort of reasonable pattern. Being able to order thoughts into rational form is a learned skill. Good trial lawyers have it. So do most scientists. Chess and go players also have the ability to see order in things where, to the untrained observer, there is none.

I had learned the trick by doing year after year of lectures. Complex or simple topics, I could always boil them down into hour segments, and then within each hour keep the discussion moving along a certain track. Good note takers in my classes always ended up with clear outlines of the material that needed to be covered. It was a trick I hadn't used in years. Not much need while marking time in a bar.

But now, with so many new things to make sense of, I tried to force my mind to drop back into that organizational frame. I had to sort out some details.

After half an hour, I had the questions and events organized into four main areas. First, I had come to help Fred and Constance get rid of a ghost so that they could keep their new lodge afloat in a way they would like. No solution yet. Even with the mirror and the disappearance of Susan, the ghost was no closer to leaving than before.

Second, I now believed that the ghost did exist and was waiting for someone named Alex to return. The ghost believed that even though eighty years had passed, Alex was still alive. That fact was interesting, considering Alex's probable age. Of course, as Steven said, ghosts seldom are in touch with the current time.

Third, Susan had come here looking for something and that something had turned out to be the very same mirror the ghost had focused on. That Susan said she was from the future and had enemies was either believable or not. However, if there were others looking for the mirror, they might show up. I didn't much like that thought, but Susan had said others would want to use it soon.

Fourth, Susan had clearly done something to the ghost's mirror and disappeared. There seemed to be no way of knowing where she went, short of triggering the mirror and following her.

All four points crossed and crisscrossed and all ended up boiling down to one simple thing. The mirror.

Yet the biggest questions surrounded the mirror.

So, I had a fifth main section. What was the mirror? Susan had said it was a random selector device planted by what she called Seeders. If that was the case, where did the Seeders come from? And how were they planting devices like the mirror at the turn of the century?

There seemed to be no clear answers, especially sitting here in a cemetery. If anything was to be done to help Fred and Constance, then answers were needed. And it followed that the only way to get those answers was to trigger the mirror and see where it took me.

There. I had finally got to the point that I knew I had to get to the minute Susan disappeared. I had to follow her. Simple and crazy as that.

For the next few minutes I sat and thought about being buried beside Carla and how important that had become to me in the last few years. If I followed Susan through the mirror, there was almost certain chance I would never make it back. In eighty years, Alex hadn't. But there was a chance I would. Alex hadn't had Susan to help him eighty years ago. She seemed to know a lot about what she was doing.

But was Susan right? Or was she crazier than I was becoming? I kept picturing her sitting there in that big old chair one moment and then gone the next. If I had to place a wager right now, I would bet on her telling the truth. I didn't like that bet.

There was only one way to find out. I stood, brushed off my pants, and headed back down the trail.

***

Constance was sitting beside Fred on the main living room couch, talking to Steven as he paced up and down in front of the fireplace.

"Ghosts don't lie," he said. "From everything we know about spirits, it would be impossible for a ghost to purposely tell a lie. At times ghosts have been mislead by the passage of events since their death. But no, I would stake anything that a deliberate falsehood would not be possible."

I dropped down onto the couch in front of the coffee table and the mirror. "What's that about?"

Constance shrugged. "I asked Steven if there's any chance that Gretchen was lying about Alex being still alive."

Steven shook his head. "No way. As far as she is concerned, and as far as I can feel by being in contact with her, Alex is still very much alive."

"He'd be at least a hundred years old," I said.

Fred nodded. "At least." He stood and handed me an old eight-by-ten framed picture. "That's one of the pictures we had copied down at the historical society and used to decorate the cabins with. Read the inscription on the back."

I glanced at the picture of seven men standing in what looked to be ankle deep mud in front of a large white tent. There was a sign hung across the peak of the tent: ATTORNEYS HOLBERG & WINSTON. In the background were some of the main buildings of the town. The last thing I wanted to look at was that dead town. I needed another drink.

I flipped the picture over. In Constance's printing it said, *Roosevelt's first law office.*

"It also had names on the original," Constance said, "but I didn't think to copy them down. I do remember that the shortest man there, the one on the left, was named Alex. They put that he was from Boston in parentheses beside his name. That's why I remembered it."

"You think that man was Gretchen's Alex?"

"Possible," Fred said. "Look how old he looks there. Must be at least thirty."

I studied the picture. At least thirty. Maybe more.

"So that makes him one hundred and ten," I said. "Makes the chance of him being alive very doubtful and answers none of the questions."

"Do you think anything is going to?" Constance asked.

"Someone following Susan would," I said.

"I knew it," Fred said, standing and moving around the couch toward the liquor cabinet. "I knew that was what you were thinking. Damn it all to hell."

"You aren't really?" Constance's eyes were wide and staring at me.

I shrugged, but that was as good as screaming a yes to her.

"I won't allow it," she said with a coldness I hadn't seen from her in years. "This lodge is not worth risking anyone's life for. No more than we've already done by having you two make that stupid dive."

Fred fixed himself a drink and returned to leaning against the log wall beside the fireplace. "She's right. We can get by with the ghost. We'll just warn people, that's all."

"Hang on a minute. Why don't we all sit down and talk about this? Let me tell you what I'm thinking and then maybe together we can come up with a better idea. All right?"

Fred nodded and sat down right where he was on the floor, with his back against the log wall.

Steven came over and sat down in the big overstuffed chair Susan had used. For a split second, I wanted to warn him to not sit there in case Susan came back, but then realized how stupid that was.

For the next few minutes, I outlined my five-point summary of the situation, ending with the fact that we had pretty good circumstantial evidence that the mirror worked once in 1909 and we witnessed the mirror working this morning. That alone added a lot of weight to Susan's future new world story.

"But that still doesn't make it safe," Constance said.

"And besides," Fred said, "there's good evidence that coming back ain't so easy."

"So then let me do it," Steven said. I glanced over at him. He hadn't said much the entire day. But I could tell his eyes were blazing with the type of adventure and curiosity that I used to feel before making a dive into a new lake.

"It's logical," he said. "I'm single, have very little family, and am a scientist. The possibilities of this are endless."

"No," I said firmly. "If anyone is going to trigger that thing again, it will be me."

"And why's that?" Steven said. "It makes no—"

"Because I found it. Simple as that."

"Hang on here a minute," Fred said. "Before we go racing to kill ourselves, let's at least try to think this through a little more."

"Good idea," I said and Steven took a deep breath and sat back in the chair.

It was silent in the room for a few moments until I turned to Steven. "Is there anything more that you've gotten from Gretchen that you haven't told us?"

Steven shrugged. "Nothing except that when I saw the picture I knew Alex was from Boston…and that Gretchen didn't consider herself a good woman."

I glanced down at the picture on the couch beside me. So that might be Alex after all. I understood what he meant about the "good woman" distinction that divided turn-of-the-century society. Gretchen had been a saloon girl, or as they were called then, a prostitute.

"Do you suppose she knew where Alex got the mirror?" Fred asked.

My mind reeled at what the answer could be. Whoever had been doing the mirrors had been around for a long time. A long time. I didn't like that thought.

"Could you tell if she was in contact with Alex?" Fred asked.

"She believes he is still alive," Steven said, his voice heavy. "But I haven't been able to tell if she had any sense of here and now."

"Same damn problem," I said to Fred and he nodded. The silence and the chill hung over the room while we thought about what to do next. I looked at Fred and Constance, then back to Steven. "Think of anything more?"

Steven laughed a strained laugh. "I know the name of the song she plays. It's called 'Tonight Has a Thousand Tomorrows.' It was Alex's favorite song."

Constance closed her eyes and shivered.

I felt the same thing. Uncontrollable shivers did a dance along my spine and right up into the back of my neck. A lovely feeling if you're into that sort of thing. I personally was getting damned tired of it.

To be continued…

USA *Today* Bestselling Writer

DEAN WESLEY SMITH

THE CASE OF THE MAN WHO SAW

A Pilgrim Hugh Incident

Pilgrim Hugh loved tough cases. He considered himself the best private detective in the Pacific Northwest, maybe the country.

He solved most cases within minutes of arriving on the scene.

But when faced with a case of a man who saw things, Pilgrim Hugh seemed stumped.

Even for Pilgrim, sometimes the obvious might not be the answer.

THE CASE OF THE MAN WHO SAW
A Pilgrim Hugh Incident

THE FIVE-LANE road cutting through the small city of Tigard outside of Portland, Oregon, was as busy as it always was during the day. Stoplights at every long block, constant stop-and-go traffic, and hundreds of businesses on both sides of the street, from pet shops to thrift stores to restaurants and fast-food standards. You could find almost everything along this ten-mile stretch of highway if you were willing to wait in the traffic long enough.

And at all the stoplights.

Pilgrim usually avoided the highway at all costs. Not today.

Pilgrim Hugh wasn't even driving his stretch limo and the traffic lights had annoyed him. He couldn't even imagine what they were doing to Donna Marks, his assistant and driver.

Donna had short brown hair and wide brown eyes and when smiling she could light up a room. She was divorced, thirty, and an expert on computers, high-speed driving, and weapons. And when annoyed, she could swear like a mythological sailor. He hadn't heard any swearing from her on the way out the Tigard highway, so that meant she was in a good mood today. Always a good thing for a woman as smart and good with guns as she was.

She had only been with him for three months now and he could no longer imagine doing this job without her help. She seemed to read his mind at times, something he actually didn't mind in the slightest.

Today she had arrived to work in tight brown shorts, a white blouse, and tennis shoes. He wore his usual jeans, dress shirt with the sleeves rolled up, and tennis shoes. People often said they looked good together, which just made Donna shake her head and walk away in disgust.

Just after one in the afternoon, Pilgrim had been called by the Chief of Police of Tigard to help out on something very weird that had happened on or along this stretch of highway. Pilgrim liked strange and weird. He lived for cases like that and specialized in puzzles that stumped the police. He worked for free for the police forces around Portland and that's why they called him, because he had also solved every case they had called him for so far.

He considered himself to be the best private detective in the Pacific Northwest, maybe in the country. He really was that good.

His road to being a private eye had gone through a bunch of strange events. First, three of years of law school, a three year event he considered so strange he couldn't believe he survived it. Then a failed first marriage and a corporate law-firm job that proved to him, without a doubt, he sucked at being a lawyer.

Or a regular husband, for that matter.

Then his grandmother had died and left him more money than he could imagine. Failed marriage and job in his wake, the arrival of the money sent him on a year of traveling and drinking, mostly drinking, which got really boring.

So back to school he went to become a private detective because he liked mystery novels and it sounded cool. Even before he hung out his PI shingle, it had become very clear that being a private eye wasn't what the novels described. The job was all computer work and long boring hours of nothingness.

He bored easily, no big surprise to anyone who knew him. He needed some excitement and challenges in his life.

Law didn't do it by itself and neither did being a standard PI. And he had done enough drinking to last for a lifetime.

So he had set up Hugh and Associates, a combination law firm and private investigative firm. Then he had hired a couple great associates who took all the boring cases and made the firm lots of money. They hired even more associates that he had no desire to meet who also made him and the firm lots and lots of money.

He also bought land and homes and apartments around Portland that also made him money. His grandmother's fortune had gotten bigger even with his best efforts to drink and spend it all.

He considered that failure his best success so far.

And that's why he could offer his services free to the different police agencies on really, really difficult and interesting cases. The weirder the case, the better.

And there was seldom a day he wasn't out on one thing or another. A lot of weird stuff happened around the Portland area.

Donna parked the stretch limo that served as their remote office off to the side of a street next to a Mongolian restaurant. Two Tigard police cars were parked closer to the intersection in front of them and neither had their lights on. The drivers might have well been inside the restaurant for all Pilgrim could tell.

The street was a slight hill and a wide sidewalk went down both sides. On the west side of the street he could see out over a shallow valley filled with a Home Depot and a couple other large box stores.

He climbed out of the back of the limo as Donna climbed out of the front. She was going to have to be careful getting too close to the five lanes of traffic flashing past. Those tight brown shorts of hers left little to the imagination and would cause wrecks he was sure.

Chief Bennett climbed out of one of the police cars on the passenger side and came back to meet Pilgrim and Donna. The day was warm, but not hot and the traffic noise wasn't loud enough where they stood to be distracting.

Pilgrim shook Bennett's outstretched hand. The man was solid, about five eight, and wore a billed cap to cover his balding head. He wasn't as tall as Pilgrim, and unlike Pilgrim who somehow managed to keep himself in shape, Bennett clearly hadn't seen a gym in a long time. He now needed a new and bigger blue shirt before the buttons exploded off his stomach.

"Thanks for coming," Bennett said. "Hope I'm not wasting your time. And mine at that."

"Never a waste to put to rest a mystery," Pilgrim said. "Want to tell us what's happening?"

"Damndest thing I have heard in a while," Bennett said. "A guy by the name of Stephen Neilson is in the front patrol car. He ran into the middle of the street there in the crosswalk, shouting for people to call for help. He then went to help a person he saw there on the road."

"No one on the ground," Pilgrim said, taking the reference from Bennett's words. If there had actually been a person

in the road, Bennett would not have said, "…a person he saw there on the road."

Bennett nodded. "This Neilson guy sure was convinced there was someone injured there. No one else stopped to help him, so I don't know if others saw the body or not."

"Who called you?" Pilgrim asked.

"A couple of people saying there was a man down in the street," Bennett said, nodding. "So maybe others did see what Neilson saw."

"Go on," Pilgrim said.

"Neilson kept talking to and comforting the person he saw, shouting for people to get help. When my men showed up, Neilson was looking confused and was back on the sidewalk staring at the street. One of my men got him into the patrol car."

"No body in the street?" Pilgrim asked just to confirm that he was hearing this right.

"No body," Bennett said. "No blood or any other sign of a body either."

"Mental breakdown," Donna said. "Military or something like that?"

Bennett shook his head. "That's what we thought as well, but Neilson is an outstanding father, husband, manager at the local Walmart. Never was in the service and has had no mental problems before that we could find. My people aren't as good as you, but they aren't bad."

Bennett said that to Donna and she nodded thanks, but said nothing.

"So let me talk with Neilson for a minute," Pilgrim said.

"Be my guest," Bennett said. "I'll get him."

Bennett turned and went up to the front patrol car.

Pilgrim turned to Donna. "Check out this Neilson guy and also if there were accidents here on this corner in the recent past. It looks like a dangerous intersection."

Pilgrim glanced up as four lanes of traffic sped past seemingly far too fast.

Donna nodded and climbed into the back of the limo. She had a station there with two major computers that came up out of cabinets and surrounded her. She had to be the best at computers Pilgrim had ever seen and had no fear of finding information in any way she could. He had a hunch he knew what she was going to find this time.

Nothing concerning Neilson.

But she had to search for the information for them to be sure.

Bennett came back down the sidewalk with Neilson, who kept glancing back at the street like he had seen a ghost.

Neilson looked like an average guy, wearing tan slacks, a dress shirt, and loafers. His hair was brown and thinning and Pilgrim figured him to be about thirty.

"Is the person you saw still there?" Pilgrim asked, not even giving Bennett a chance to introduce Neilson.

"No," Neilson said, shaking his head. "Vanished just as the police arrived. But the guy had seemed so real."

"What did the victim look like?" Pilgrim asked.

"Senior guy, about eighty or so," Neilson asked. "Bald. It looked as if he had been hit by a car. Blood on the guy's blue shirt and he was twisted up. I was afraid to touch him so I just shouted for help."

Neilson looked down at his slacks as if seeing them for the first time. "I should be covered in the guy's blood because it was everywhere and I was kneeling beside him. I really wanted to help the guy."

Pilgrim had no doubt at all about that. And he had no doubt at all that Neilson wasn't the problem here, just a Samaritan stuck in this.

"Please hold on for a moment," Pilgrim said to Bennett and Neilson.

Pilgrim then went over to the limo and opened the door. "Senior male victim, pedestrian. About eighty or so. Bald."

"Copy that," Donna said as Pilgrim closed the door and turned back to Neilson.

"Am I going insane?" Neilson asked.

"In our own ways," Pilgrim said, "We all are. But in this case, you are perfectly sane and tried to help what you thought

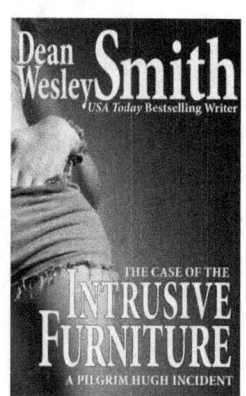

was an injured man. Nothing at all insane about that."

Neilson nodded and managed to take a deep breath and exhale. Pilgrim could see the life coming back into the man.

"You think you know what caused this?" Bennett asked.

"I am pretty sure," Pilgrim said. "But we need to wait for Donna to finish her work first."

"How long will that take?" Bennett asked.

Pilgrim smiled and turned and pointed to the limo. "About now."

At that moment Donna opened the back door and climbed out. Her brown shorts and white blouse giving all three of them a wonderful show of fantastic beauty.

Pilgrim noticed and smiled. He was sure that Neilson didn't notice at all he was so rattled, and Bennett just sucked in his breath and turned to face Pilgrim.

"Victim you were trying to help was David Luke," Donna said. "He was hit in the crosswalk by a hit-and-run driver five months ago and died in the street before help could arrive."

"How is that possible?" Neilson said. "The guy didn't look like a ghost."

"Not believing in ghosts either," Bennett said, shaking his head.

"No ghosts," Pilgrim said. He turned to Donna. "Got a few suspects."

"Auto repair shop just up the hill on the other side of the street," Donna said. "Chinese restaurant right beyond that, depending on who has the angle."

Pilgrim glanced at Bennett and Neilson. "How far into the street was the body?"

"In the crosswalk," Neilson said. "Second lane out on the east-bound side, this side."

Pilgrim nodded. "Chief Bennett, Mr. Neilson, would you please wait here while I take a walk to the corner and back."

"I'll get you both a bottle of water," Donna said turning to the limo as Pilgrim started up the sidewalk.

It took him only about thirty seconds to reach the busy street. Donna was correct, the auto repair shop up the street was a logical target, but the roof wasn't high enough for an angle over the cars in the other lanes and in the turning lane.

If he was right, the image of the body of David Luke was projected on the street by a very powerful laser projector, something only the military might have. That would take some pretty large equipment and computer power and money. The Chinese restaurant had a phony front roofline that could easily hide large equipment behind it on the building's flat roof.

And that roof was high enough to have a clear sight-line to the spot where the body appeared.

Pilgrim turned and headed back down the street. Just a little more research was needed to put the why with the how on this puzzle.

As he approached Bennett and Donna and Neilson, Pilgrim said, "Let's all climb into the limo and I'll explain while Donna tries to figure out exactly who is behind this and why."

Donna nodded and moved over to hold the door for the three men, then climbed in last.

Pilgrim took his normal seat in the back. He had a hidden computer station in his seat as well, but he saw no reason to bring it up at the moment. Bennett and Neilson both took the side seat, both marveling at the leather interior, mahogany woods, and the state-of-the-art computer system Donna had surrounding her behind the driver's seat.

Even with four people in the back of the limo, it still didn't feel crowded at all. Pilgrim loved this moving office more than he liked his penthouse office on the top of his firm.

"Chinese restaurant has the angle," Pilgrim said. "Find out why? And you might want to check their power bills. I'm guessing a laser of that size pulls some real power."

Donna nodded.

"Laser projection?" Bennett asked.

"Technology has come a long ways and images can be made to look very, very real from a distance with a direct line. At night you would have been able to see the beam, but during the day, you only saw the projected image on the ground."

"So if I had touched the guy?" Neilson asked.

"Your hand would have gone right through the image," Pilgrim said. "Just like a ghost, which is my guess why someone is doing this. I'm betting David Luke's case has not been solved, so whoever is doing this wants to haunt the intersection with his ghost."

"Got that in one," Donna said. "Hit-and-run driver never found, but we might be able to solve it if you give me a few minutes to do this other thing first."

Bennett looked at Donna, then back at Pilgrim, shaking his head.

"So I'm not going crazy," Neilson said, smiling.

"Got it," Donna said. She turned slightly to the three men. "David Luke's grandson is named David Luke as well. Luke junior has numbers of major degrees in physics and light refraction from more than one major school. His parents own the Chinese restaurant. His grandfather paid for all the years of college."

Donna turned back to the computers, her fingers moving as fast as Pilgrim had seen them move.

Pilgrim turned to Bennett. "I don't think this young David Luke has broken any laws, do you?"

"Certainly could have gotten someone hurt," Bennett said.

"True," Pilgrim said, "But other than having Neilson here question his sanity, nothing was harmed."

Bennett slowly nodded. "What do you have in mind?"

Pilgrim smiled. "I'll get him to shut the machine down and never do it again. And maybe offer him some support and a job."

"He's not going to want to stop until his grandfather's murderer is caught," Bennett said.

"Don't blame him," Neilson said.

Pilgrim smiled and pointed to a printer that had suddenly started spitting out paper from a hidden panel.

Donna took the three sheets, glanced at them, and handed them to Bennett.

"Your detective's investigation found traces of red truck paint on the victim," Donna said. "Eye witnesses also said it was a red Dodge pickup, fairly new."

"I remember that," Bennett said. "We could never find the truck."

Donna smiled. "An auto repair shop in Walla Walla, Washington, fixed damage on the front of a red Dodge pickup one week after Luke senior was killed and repainted the entire truck green. The owner of the truck that was fixed in Walla Walla lives about a half mile from here and already has three DUI convictions and a revoked driver's license."

"Shit, no wonder we couldn't find the truck," Bennett said.

"Even better news," Donna said, "The auto body shop has not yet thrown away the original bumper and front panel of the truck. They held it expecting insurance to come and investigate at some point. So I would imagine you can match evidence on the bumper to the senior Luke."

Bennett just shook his head and looked at the papers one more time, then said, "Thank you."

Then Bennett turned to Pilgrim. "You'll get the kid to turn off the laser show?"

Pilgrim smiled. "I'll do it and tell him you have a lead on his grandfather's killer thanks to his display."

Bennett turned to Neilson. "You all right?"

"My wife's never going to believe any of this," Neilson said, smiling. "But just happy that man I saw in the street will get some justice now."

"That he will," Bennett said, opening the door and climbing out.

Donna shut down her computer and retracted it as Neilson also climbed out.

Pilgrim followed Neilson and Donna got out behind him.

"Thanks again you two," Bennett said.

With that he and Neilson headed back up the street toward the two cars.

"It's a nice day." Donna said, smiling at Pilgrim. "Shall we walk up to the restaurant?"

Pilgrim laughed. "Are you kidding me? That intersection is deadly. Just get me across there and to the restaurant safely and I'll buy lunch."

"And explain to me over lunch what you meant by offering the kid a job?" Donna asked.

"Just thinking I got that big empty building near the Pearl I just bought last week," Pilgrim said. "That might be great for a research center. I will need someone with real innovation and courage of convictions to run it."

"To research what?" Donna asked.

"Damned if I know," Pilgrim said. "I just thought of the idea."

With that, Donna laughed, shook her head, and then turned to climb into the driver's seat of the limo.

Pilgrim climbed into the back and buckled up his seat belt. He loved it when he made Donna shake her head. Sometimes that was more fun than solving a case.

Or in this instance, they had solved two cases. Even better.

~

DEAN WESLEY SMITH

A BAD DAY FOR THE DREAM

A Cold Poker Gang Story

Thirty years ago in Las Vegas, Becky Penn said goodnight to her mother to go out with friends and vanished without a trace.

Retired Detectives Bayard Lott and Julia Rogers, members of the Cold Poker Gang, take on Becky Penn's cold case.

They love working with other retired detectives and playing a little poker once a week, all to solve cold cases.

A puzzle mystery unraveled carefully by the retired detectives who make up the Cold Poker Gang.

A BAD DAY FOR THE DREAM
A Cold Poker Gang Story

PROLOGUE

March 3rd, 1990
Las Vegas, Nevada

BECKY PENN TIED her long brown hair back away from her face and laughed as her mom stood in their bathroom door, arms crossed over her chest, the worried look that Becky saw so much from her.

Her mom had raised her since their father had left when Becky was three. The two of them were more like sisters at times and Becky loved that.

Becky was dressed in a light skirt, a new blouse she had just bought, and had on sandals, since the weather was already starting to warm up.

Becky's mom had already changed from her nursing scrubs into a light sweatshirt and jeans. She seldom wore shoes around the house and tonight was no exception.

"It's all right, mom," Becky said, smiling as she finished up and turned from the mirror. "Paul and I are just headed to a party just off the strip. I'm going to meet him there."

"I wish you wouldn't," her mom said, shaking her head.

"I know, I know," Becky said. "You don't like him."

"I'm not sure why you do," her mom said.

Becky laughed. Paul was a good guy who worked hard. And he was a very gentle soul. Becky liked that about him.

Becky kissed her mother lightly on the cheek as she went past and out into the hallway toward the front door. "You worry too much."

"Sometimes I wish you worried more," her mom said.

Then both of them laughed. That exchange had happened for every date Becky had ever gone on from a freshman in high school and all the way through four years at UNLV. It made them both feel better.

"Don't wait up," Becky said.

A minute later she was in her red two-door Toyota and headed out toward the Strip.

It was the last time anyone saw her. She just simply vanished.

And just like so many other missing persons, after no leads came up, her case went cold.

Thirty years cold.

ONE

*April 10th, 2020
Las Vegas, Nevada*

RETIRED DETECTIVE BAYARD Lott ran a hand through his short white hair and sighed. They weren't supposed to find a body. Lott hated every time they did that. It was never the way they wanted to close missing person's cases. But more often than not, it was exactly how they closed them.

"Looks like we found Becky," Retired Detective Julia Rogers said.

Julia stood beside Lott staring down at the skeleton that was slowly emerging from the desert sand and dirt where it had been buried for almost thirty years, as far as they could tell.

Julia had on a light white blouse and a sports bra under it. She wore jeans and tennis shoes and a wide-brimmed white golf hat to keep the sun off her face.

Lott had on a short-sleeved dress shirt, jeans, tennis shoes and a wide-brimmed Panama hat. They had expected to spend time in the sun in the desert to the north of Las Vegas, so they were both also smeared with sunscreen that smelled like they belonged on a beach instead of out in the desert.

They might have looked silly and smelled funny, but he was in his mid-sixties and Julia in her late fifties and they were smart enough to take no chances. At their age, too much sun did not do well on either of them.

The open grave in front of them was being carefully worked by a couple of Las Vegas police's best forensic lab people. They were in white suits that had to be hot in the morning April sun in the desert. And they were being very careful to brush away sand and then shovel it into containers to be sifted.

Lott could visualize the wonderful college graduation picture of Becky Penn. She had been a beautiful woman with a promising future. She vanished on March 3rd, 1990, on her way to a party to meet her boyfriend.

It was her boyfriend, Paul Vaughan, that had reported to Becky's mother three hours after they were supposed to meet that Becky had not shown up. He had called concerned that Becky had been sick or something.

Her mother filed a missing person's report.

Nothing had ever come of it. The detective assigned to the case did some fine interviews, found nothing.

Two months ago, Retired Detective Andor Williams brought the thin file on Becky Penn's case to the weekly meeting of the Cold Poker Gang.

Lott loved the weekly sessions in his card room in his house. Retired detectives got together, played poker, and talked about cold cases. Then during the week between games, they worked the cold cases.

The Las Vegas Chief of Police had given the Cold Poker Gang special status to carry badges and guns because they had solved so many cold cases and wanted no credit for any of it.

For the retired detectives, it was just the sense of feeling valued that mattered and continuing at their own pace, without paperwork, the job they had loved for decades.

When Julia joined the group, she had retired from Reno because of a shattered bone in her leg where she had been shot. For almost two years, she was the only woman in the gang until six months ago two of Las Vegas's best women detectives had retired. Both had taken a month vacation and then joined the group.

Now the Cold Poker Gang often had seven or eight people at the table on a Tuesday night. There were eleven official members and every detective on the force liked helping them.

At any given moment, the gang might have eight or nine cold cases they were working in some fashion or another.

"Let's sit in the car for awhile," Julia said, turning from the grave.

Lott agreed to that idea. The sun was getting warmer by the minute and there was absolutely nothing they could do to help in that shallow hole. Getting Becky Penn's remains out of that hole would take time and painstaking work. Lott was just glad he wasn't doing the work, especially in one of those white suits they wore these days.

Lott got his white Cadillac SUV started and the air-conditioning running as Julia dug them both out a cold bottle of water from the ice chest sitting on the back seat.

Then they just sat in silence for a moment, cooling down and watching the two men in the shallow hole work.

Lott was always surprised at how wonderful cold water tasted after being out in the Nevada sun for a while.

"I can't believe we found her," Julia said after a moment.

"We're still not one hundred percent it is her," Lott said.

And they weren't, but that was just a technical issue now. They had figured out where she was buried exactly from notes in a journal left by her boyfriend, Paul Vaughan, when he killed himself twenty years ago.

From what they could tell when they got the journal, still stored with Paul's things by his sister, that he and Becky had gotten into a fight and he had killed her.

The journal went on to give exact directions to where he had buried her and then what he had done to cover his crime.

Lott had found the writing creepy. Impassionate while being angry. Paul blamed Becky's death on her, taking no responsibility at all.

Lott had been upset that the guy was dead. But if he hadn't been dead, there was no telling if they ever would have solved Becky's cold case. They were lucky in a couple of ways. That he was dead and that his sister had just stored what few things he owned in boxes in her basement.

But something felt off to both Julia and Lott. And Lott couldn't put his finger

on it at all. First, they had no idea why a killer like Paul would write down what he had done, then give exact directions to the grave.

And his sister had told them that Paul hated to write anything, let alone in a journal.

But it seemed, at least on the surface, that Paul had started the journal when he and Becky started dating and they had confirmed with Becky's mother some of the dates and times in the journal as best as she could remember.

So it all seemed real enough.

The second thing that seemed off was no one knew what had happened to Becky's red Toyota. The car had simply vanished and Paul made no mention of it in his strange journal. And he should have.

Getting rid of that car had to be a lot harder than burying her in the desert.

Something was off on all of this, but darned if Lott could figure out what was bothering him about it all.

Then, in front of them, one of the two men in white suits working in the shallow grave stood up, turned and waved for Lott and Julia to come over.

Then both men climbed out of the shallow grave and one headed for their vehicle, pulling off his white suit as he went.

"Something went wrong," Julia said as both she and Lott climbed out of the car.

The other man who had waved them over had pulled off the top of his white suit as well and was working on a bottle of water. His face was covered in sweat.

"What did you find?" Lott asked.

The guy just pointed for them to look into the grave and kept drinking.

It took a moment for Lott to see it, but then he did.

Nowhere in any report did it say that Becky had three arms.

"There's another body with her," Julia said softly.

"Shit," Lott said. "Just shit."

TWO

April 12th, 2020
Las Vegas, Nevada

LOTT SET THE bucket of Kentucky Fried Chicken on his kitchen table while Julia pulled out three bottles of water from the fridge. Andor had just parked outside in the driveway and was going to join them for lunch.

The smell of the chicken filled Lott's remodeled kitchen. In the remodel two years ago, he had put in the best counters, all new cabinets and flooring, and new appliances. But the floor plan of the kitchen was exactly as it had been when he and his wife had lived here.

His wife of thirty years had died of cancer almost five years before and it wasn't until Julia walked into his life that he could ever imagine enjoying the company of another woman. But now he did.

So now he and Julia and Andor, Lott's former partner back on the force before they both had retired to take care of sick wives, formed a team.

And outside of the nights with the Cold Poker Gang playing cards, the three of them often met over KFC in Lott's kitchen to talk over cases.

But Lott had a hunch today wasn't going to be much of a good lunch, no matter how wonderful the bucket of KFC smelled. The topic was Becky Penn's case.

Lott spread around three paper plates and Julia got some forks for pulling the hot chicken apart and some spoons for the sides that came with the bucket. They didn't often eat much of the sides. All three of them just loved the fresh chicken.

Lott came in the back door, his solid frame and balding head moving like a bull. He had a cold towel around his neck and was sweating.

Julia handed him a fresh towel to wipe off his face and head and neck, then she sat next to Lott at the table.

Andor dropped some files at the back of the table and all three of them dug into the chicken.

Finally, after pretty much demolishing his first piece and starting on a second, Lott couldn't take it any longer.

He looked at Andor. "Well, was one of them Becky Penn?"

When the other body was found in Becky's grave, the case had reverted back to the regular younger detectives. By the end of the day, the techs doing the digging had found a total of four bodies in that grave, all stacked on one another with a very thin layer of dirt between them.

From what Lott had heard, they were now doing ground radar sweeps around the grave to see if others were buried close by.

Paul Vaughan's journal had led them to the location, but he had said nothing about killing and burying other women.

Andor nodded, wiping chicken grease off his mouth with a paper towel. "It was Becky on top," Andor said. "Confirmed by remnants of what she was wearing, hair color, and the remains of her id buried with her. They will run some DNA tests, but no one is doubting it is her."

"And the other three?" Julia asked.

"They don't have a clue," Andor said. "But they are treating all three as live murder cases at the moment."

"Three?" Lott asked.

Again Andor nodded. "They are closing Becky's case. Seems we solved another cold case."

Lott glanced at Julia who was shaking her head. He felt the same way. Becky's case was far, far from closed.

Andor just looked at them. "We're out of this one for now. You both know that, don't you?"

Lott knew they were. As long as the younger detectives considered the three other bodies open and live murder cases, there was nothing anyone retired in the Cold Poker Gang could do.

And actually, by doing anything, they might jeopardize the entire existence of the Cold Poker Gang.

They worked cold cases. Period.

That was the firm rule the Chief of Police had put on them.

Becky's case was officially closed and the other three were live murder cases.

The Cold Poker Gang was done with them.

Julia was nodding, and not looking happy.

Lott just sat there, not even interested in another piece of cold chicken.

"This day just sucks," Lott said.

"Yeah, it does," Andor said. "But we have to give the hotshot young detectives a crack at this first. Remember, we were young once as well."

"Speak for yourself," Julia said. "I'm still young, thank you very much."

Lott and Andor both laughed.

Julia smiled. "Not sure how I should take that laughing."

"Oh, oh," Andor said, winking at Lott.

"So what are the files?" Julia asked, indicating the folding files that Andor had at the top of the table.

"I brought them for storage here," he said, starting into another piece of chicken.

Lott laughed at that. He knew what they were without even asking. After the decades of the two of them working together, Lott knew how his partner thought.

Lott had Julia hand them to him and then without looking at their contents, he stood and put them in an empty cabinet above the fridge.

Storage.

"All four files for the bodies in the grave?" Julia asked, starting to catch on.

Andor nodded. "I'll get more from downtown and update them as the young hotshots find information."

Lott laughed and sat down and took another piece of chicken.

"And if they solve the cases?" Julia asked.

Lott laughed. "If they solve them like they think we solved Becky's murder, then we go to work on all four of the cases."

"And if they don't solve them, then we go to work on the cases," Andor said, smiling. "But that's going to be years down the road I'm afraid."

Lott nodded. "So the day officially sucks. We are officially fired from these cases."

"We move on," Julia said, nodding and taking another piece of chicken.

"We move on," Andor said, wiping chicken juice from his face again.

"There are no shortages of cold cases for us to solve," Julia said.

"Amen to that," Andor said.

Lott knew that was the truth. But he just hated failing, hated having a case taken from him, hated everything about this.

The Cold Poker Gang hadn't really solved a cold case. They had just found more murders that, more than likely, would turn into cold cases in a year or two.

Lott knew that all three of them hated failing. They didn't volunteer their time in their retirement to fail.

But sometimes it happened. Sometimes even the Cold Poker Gang failed.

Or, as they say in poker, you can't win every hand, even on good nights.

But down the road, way down the road, they just might get to play this hand again.

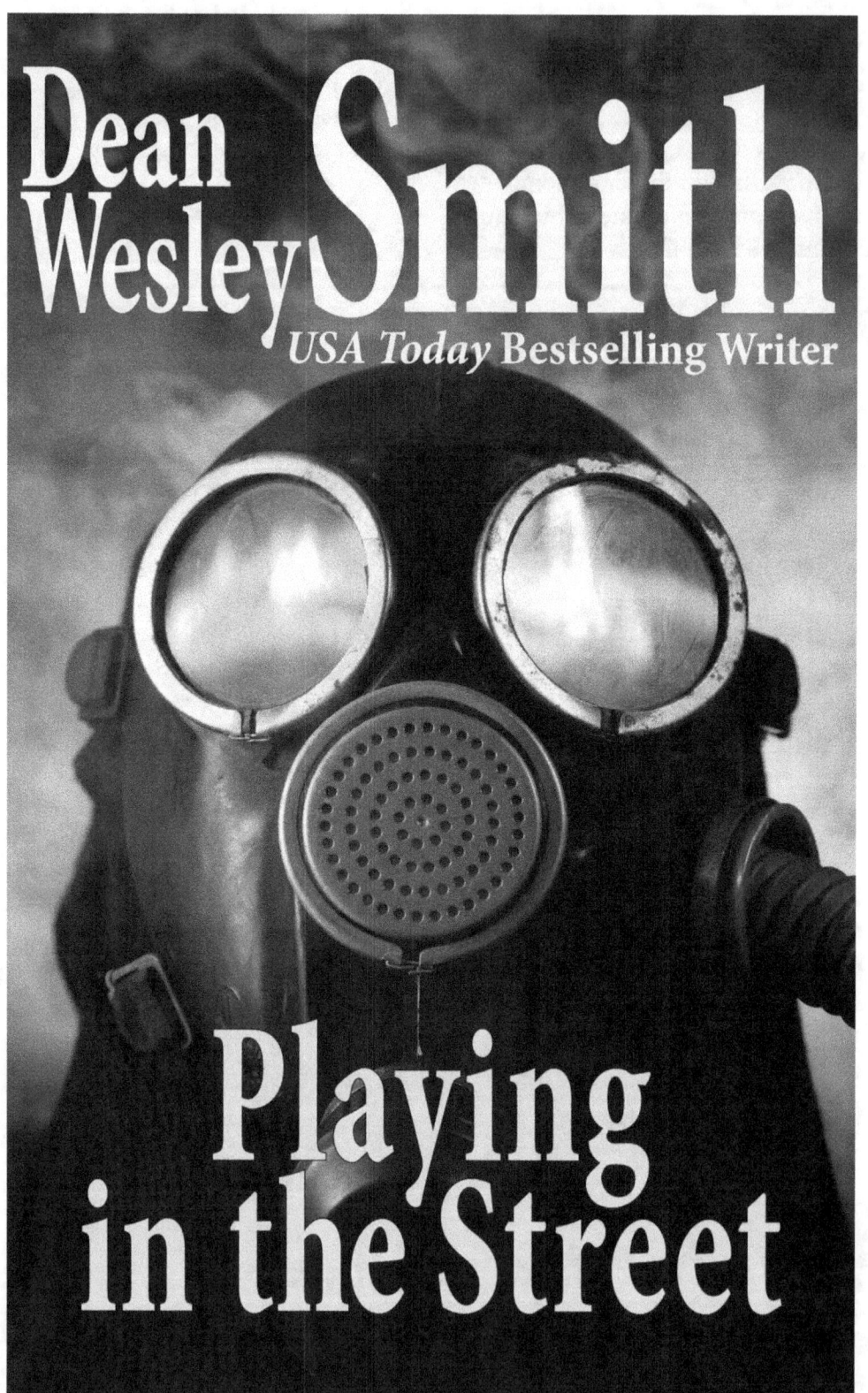

Dean Wesley Smith

USA Today Bestselling Writer

Playing in the Street

Sometimes a lost gold mine offers up more than just gold.

And sometimes a secret should remain a secret.

A science fiction short story that ranges from early Idaho to the future, telling the story of family and a lost gold mine.

A version of this story first appeared in The Secret Prophecies of Nostradamus, edited by Cynthia Sternau and Martin H. Greenberg.

PLAYING IN THE STREET

ONE

Moscow, Idaho
July, 2030

A FINE LAYER of gray dust covered everything. Old cars, rusted, tires flat, lined the street like a huge metal fence. Every car coated with the dust. No animal footprints, not even that of a cat crawling on the hood and sleeping in the sun. Nothing since the gray dust fell.

Litter had spilled out of a garbage can in front of one house and was now glued in place by the dust. The trees were dead, black skeletons, making the street appear to be in the grip of winter all year long. A stop light at the street's end, three dark round eyes in the sky, watched the complete lack of movement on the quiet suburban scene. It watched the mailboxes and the child's bike. It watched the basketball hoop above the garage door of the split-level and the bare areas that had once been green yards.

Before. The evidence of before was all along the street. It lined the street. It was the street. There had been a time of life here before the dust had settled over it. The dust had fallen at night, then it had rained and the dust had become hard, like a child's clay exposed to the air too long. It still looked mostly like a layer of gray dust, but it never altered. Not even the winter snows and spring melts could move or change it. And there was nothing anyone could do to clean it up. The dust was there to stay for centuries to come, of that there was no doubt.

The unblinking glass eyes of the old, rusted cars watched silently as the dust held its stranglehold on the neighborhood.

Now there was only silence.

Now there was only now.

And dust.

I am always careful to walk in my own footsteps. The boots of my protective suit leave large, patterned prints in the top thin layer of dust and I am careful on this street to match those prints step for step. Not doing so would feel as if I was tearing up a piece of my own history.

I always park my government van near the old grocery store and start down the street under the stoplight, keeping to the inside of the sidewalk. Seven houses down from the light is a light blue, two-story house, with a two-car garage. An average house for this neighborhood and this part of the little city.

But this house is special.

Through the door is an open wood foyer. Beyond that a plush living room and then beyond that a dining room with oak tables, dishes in glass cabinets, and an empty fruit bowl in the middle of the table. Everything looks so dated, yet so familiar, as if I have just stepped into a time machine and gone back twenty years.

The rugs are rotted, the drapes hang partially ripped from the hooks by age and their own weight, and the normal dust of the years gives everything a washed out look. But the living room is still a beautiful sight to me; comfortable and yet elegant.

There is a brick fireplace against the wall opposite the front door. On the mantel of that fireplace is a picture, faded slightly, but still clear under the glass of its frame.

It is a picture of three children playing in the street in front of the house. Playing a game of catch with a football between the rows of parked cars and in the small green front yards. In the background beyond the stoplight a car is caught in the frozen motion of the now of the picture. There is no dust, so the colors of the picture are bright, vibrant in their life.

The three children are smiling and the cars are mostly clean. It is a picture of a street that feels like home. The children feel comfortable playing there. I remember, since I am in that picture. I am the one with the football. I was twelve. I was comfortable and happy and alive, even though at the time I never thought of it in those terms.

The picture was taken many summers before Grandpa died and everything changed.

But I remember the time when the picture was taken, everything about life seemed enjoyable along that street. I give the street far more good times than bad. But that too may be nothing more than my memory coloring and adding to the scene in the picture. Sometimes I wonder.

Beside that picture on the fireplace mantel is another picture. This picture is an older one, more faded, of a young couple standing on the steps in front of the same house. She is dressed as a bride. He a groom.

Both are smiling and his arm is around her waist, holding her while she holds a large bouquet of flowers. In the reflection of the picture window behind and to the right of them is a clear picture of the street. People are standing in the driveway and on the sidewalk beside the unplanted yard. There are two empty fields across the street where houses are not yet built. The street and the neighborhood are both very young, almost as young as the smiling couple.

They are my parents. They used to live in this home.

They are still here, in bed upstairs, two skeletons covered with the dust of years. The real dust outside caught them while they slept, as it did most of this city. They died not knowing that death was floating down on them.

I consider them lucky. But it is still hard standing at the foot of that bed, looking at their skeletons. I have done so a hundred times and will probably do so another hundred.

My mother, Mrs. Richard Gilet, Dot to her friends, was still a slim woman at fifty when she died. Her arm was draped across my father's chest. I find that to be a sign that they were happy the night they died. Richard Gilet, Rich to his friends, was sleeping on his back, one arm raised over his head above the pillow. The bone of that arm holds what is left of his hair in place. What is left of Mother's dark brown hair has dropped in a bunch around the top of her pillow. The sheets and quilt were pulled up to mid chest level and their remains make very little dent under the quilt.

I am glad I did not come in here until many years after the dust. I do not think I could have stood in this room, imagining that I could smell them rotting in the summer heat through my protective suit. I am glad that the air has already taken their eyes and their skin and left the bones and hair. It is better that way.

With them as only skeletons I can still sometimes retrieve the memories of bouncing on the bed to wake them on Christmas morning. I can still remember them that morning; sleepy, smiling, the

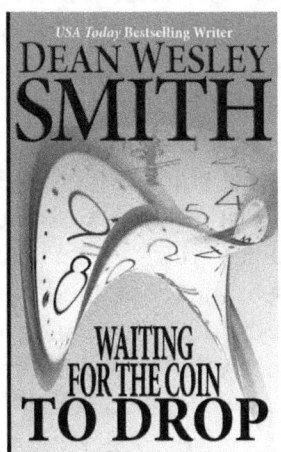

smell of them filling the room. Sometimes the memory is so strong I want to jump on the bed again to wake them.

But I do not. I need the reality of them sleeping here after death much more than I need the quick release of jumping on the bed and messing up their last scene.

At least so far. But at times that urge to jump into bed with them is very strong. Someday I may fail to resist it.

I am now older than my father was. I find life interesting that with the dust and everything since the dust, I am still here. I really don't understand what brings me to this room time after time. I have yet to visit my own room, just down the hall. I loved my own room. It was always a safe place for me.

Yet I always just visit here, in my parents' bedroom, always careful to remain in my own footprints and not move fast enough to mess anything up.

It seems odd that I have access to this small city, this frozen museum of a life twenty years past. This is a city of death. In my lifetime, and for many lifetimes to follow, no human or animal will be able to live here or walk here unprotected. But since I am the one who told the world, who gave the history of it all, who knows the most about what happened, the government sees fit to let me in.

I suppose they understand that someday I will open the protective suit and stay with my parents. But that is never talked about and for the moment they are happy to let me in and have me report back on what little I see. I am one of the very few crazy enough to even want to be here.

Yet because of my father and his father, I know what happened to this small city. And I know I feel responsible.

Somehow I should have tried to stop them. I knew we didn't know enough. I knew we should have reported our findings to the government and gotten help. But I was still fairly young and just out of graduate school and my voice and my worries were not enough to stop them. My father and the others had been so sure of themselves. So sure they understood. So sure that the understanding would take them places they never imagined.

I looked at the skeletons of my sleeping parents. Maybe this trip down the street was the right time to open up my protective suit and join them.

I stood there in the same exact spot where I always stood, staring at their last embrace.

Not yet. Maybe next time.

TWO

Boise, Idaho
March 14, 1913

IDAHO GOVERNOR FRANK Stunenburg dropped down out of the passenger seat of the Model T. He stood thin and tall, almost too tall for a westerner. He had sharp, dark eyes and a smile that disarmed even his most staunch detractors. He brushed the dust off his well-worn suit and turned back to retrieve a package from beside the seat that contained material his wife had asked him to pick up. "Thanks, John," he yelled to the Attorney General over the loud sputtering of the engine. "Going to have to get me one of these since they built the Governor's mansion way out here."

"That you are, Frank." John waved and swung the Model T around and started it bumping down the dirt road back toward the center of town. The Governor watched, thinking that sometimes he wished things weren't moving so fast. He enjoyed horses and always had. Riding in those automobiles was hard on the kidneys. But technology was moving fast. Too fast. And when the world heard about the discovery under that mountain outside of Moscow, it would move even faster.

He shook his head. He still wasn't going to believe what they had told him until he got up there and took a look for himself.

He sighed. It had been a hard day all the way around. Actually a hard month, with the union mining problems up North. He wished like hell they could have just included that part of the state in the Montana territory. But they hadn't. Back East it had all been political compromise with no attention to how difficult it was to move from the southern part of Idaho to the northern.

So as Governor he was stuck with the unions and the problems and all the killing going on in a place that took five days during the summer to get to and was impossible to travel to in the winter. Somehow the killing and the union had to be stopped. But no one seemed to know just how to do it. He had come down hard anti-union and that stance had divided the legislature in Boise. A fist-fight had even broken out yesterday on the House floor.

He could hardly wait to see what the legislators would do with the Moscow discovery.

Frank looked up at the not completely finished mansion and the young trees that surrounded it. It felt good to be home, even though they had only lived here a short time.

Someday he knew the new mansion would be a place where Idaho governors would be proud to live. But it too had caused a huge amount of resentment between the people in the north and the government in Boise in the south. Northerners were still fuming over the theft of the state seal from the northern city of Lewiston and the government's move to Boise. It had been a midnight raid and a three day non-stop ride over twenty years ago. But it wasn't anywhere near forgotten.

Between the Moscow discovery, the seat of government and the union problems in the northern mines, he would be lucky to keep the young state in one piece over the next few years.

A new white fence ran across the front of the mansion and down the left side. A stream and a grove of maple trees bordered the right side. It was a beautiful setting above the growing main city. The government planners had been right to build it here. He was proud to be its first resident.

Frank hefted the package and started for the front gate. For the last month the gate had stood wide open, held that way by a large rock. But now it was closed. Frank thought nothing of it.

He switched his wife's package to his left hand, flipped the latch up on the gate, and pulled.

The explosion sent most of the Governor of Idaho flying back into the middle of the road and left a crater the size of a house in front of the new governor's mansion.

THREE

North of Moscow, Idaho
October 6, 1999

"Your grandfather's notes say it is about here," my dad said as he pushed aside underbrush and climbed over a small ridge of rock. I looked up at the red back of dad's hunting jacket as he picked his way up through the pine trees and underbrush. I couldn't believe I was with him on this crazy treasure hunt. We were a good half mile up the mountain above Grandpa's house and I was beginning to think we were going to be lost. Or worse, shot by a stupid deer hunter who thought

our crashing through the brush was a reason to shoot.

It was bad enough that my crazy grandfather had died, especially right in the middle of my senior football season and the roughest semester I had signed up for in four years. But now dad was acting like a strange kid since he found Grandpa's journal.

Three hours ago Dad had been up in the attic cleaning out and sorting Grandpa's things. When he came down he looked as if he had seen a ghost. Mom asked him if he was all right and he handed her a yellow paper and then a journal that had Gold Mine written on the outside in gold pen. He said it was Grandpa's handwriting.

"Take a look at this," Dad said, and sat down at the kitchen table where Grandpa used to sit and smoke. The house still held the thick, rich smell of his pipe smoke, but with the windows open and the cool fall air from the surrounding forest coming in, the place was almost bearable.

I crowded in behind Mom and we both read. The first entry in the journal said that Grandpa and Grandma had moved to Moscow from Boise back in 1914 to find a lost gold mine.

Dad flipped quickly ahead in the journal. Grandpa and Grandma had lived in Moscow and a large number of the entries for the next year tell about Grandpa's search for the mine. In May of 1915 his journal says he found the abandoned mine on the back side of Moscow Mountain. But the mouth of the mine had caved in and he would need money and time to dig it out. He was going to very quietly check around town to see if anyone had a claim filed. For some reason that entry seemed almost paranoid.

The next entry in the journal a week later was about how much trouble he would have getting a claim to the land because the previous owner had disappeared years before under very strange circumstances.

Next entry was very short. "May have mentioned the mine to the wrong person."

There was another short entry a month later about meeting a man named Carl and the other members of the Wheelbarrow Association. The entry said they were the ones who had collapsed the entrance to the old mine, called the Lost Wheelbarrow Mine. Grandpa said in the entry that he had dinner with the men of the association and there was no way they were going to allow him to open the mine back up.

He feared for his and Grandma's life, since it was obvious these men would do anything to keep the mine closed. And had numbers of times before.

The last entry was a month later. All it said was, "They took me inside the mine. Now I understand. Joined the Association. Youngest member. Let us hope I will be the last."

Then in a different color ink Grandpa had scratched, "I was right about the Governor."

There was nothing else in the journal except a deed showing that Grandpa owned a huge chunk of the back side of Moscow Mountain and a map drawn years later after Grandmother had died in 1965. Grandpa had built a house on the back side of Moscow Mountain the next year. The map gave exact directions to the mine from the house. The location on the map of the mine was inside the land that Grandpa owned and the deed gave clear ownership of the Lost Wheelbarrow Mine to Grandpa. And now Dad. Grandpa had scratched on the side of the deed, "No gold left."

By the time Mom and I finished reading, Dad could hardly contain himself. He had never heard Grandpa talk at all about the mine or why Grandpa and Grandma had moved to Moscow or why Grandpa had moved to the back of Moscow Mountain. It just hadn't occurred to Dad to ask. In fact Dad had no idea that Grandpa had owned so much forest land.

Dad wanted to go see if we could find the mine and Mom wanted nothing to do with it. So Mom decided to keep cleaning while Dad and I went up the mountain looking for the old mine sight. It was a wild goose chase, as far as I was concerned, but Mom wouldn't let Dad go alone because he had had heart pains last year. I was elected.

Dad scrambled over the top of a slight ridge and disappeared through some underbrush. A moment later I heard him say, "Got it." Then, as if I hadn't been right behind him the entire time he yelled "Gary, it's over here."

I ducked under brush and around a large pine and came out into a slight clearing about fifty yards wide. It looked as if someone had kept the trees and brush cut back. Across the clearing in front of me the mountain side went up sharply and there was a rock outcropping to the right. Even with the growth of brush under the outcropping I could see where a long time before there had been a cut into the side of the hill. Dad was standing in front of the cut, looking through the brush.

I moved up beside him. "Any opening?" I asked.

Dad shook his head. "Doesn't look like it." He broke back some limbs and climbed around where the opening should have been. After a minute he said, "No luck."

He backed out into the clearing and stood looking around. "Your grandfather must have kept this area cut back for some reason. It looks as if there are the remains of a road coming in here." I looked to the right where he had pointed. It still took me a moment to see the faint possibility of a road cut into the hillside, now overgrown with sixty-year-old trees.

Granted, it was fascinating thinking that way back in the past someone had dug a mine here. It was sort of thrilling to think there was some mystery about it that Grandpa had kept to himself. But mostly right then I was worried about passing a City Planning test tomorrow morning and then making it through football practice at three. I had already missed three practices because of Grandpa's death.

"Dad. Mind if we head back now?"

He stood for a moment, hands on hips, staring at the cut in the mountain, nodding. "No problem," he said. "But guess where I'm going to spend next summer?"

"Water-skiing behind our new boat?"

He laughed. "Well, just maybe. We might buy one. Right after I open up this old mine."

He started off down the hill before I even had a chance to groan. I knew for a fact I was going to get stuck helping him.

FOUR

Moscow, Idaho
October 17, 1999

ACTUALLY IT WAS while I was standing under a hot shower trying to clear some of the aches from grueling football practice that I figured out how to get into Grandpa's old mine. Grandpa himself had told us in his journal, but we just hadn't seen it.

Since we had found the journal Dad had become a different man. He was pricing equipment for digging and making all sorts of plans to get inside that mountain. He and I had been back up there twice and his excitement was starting to be catching. I found myself daydreaming about it in class and now standing in the shower after practice I figured out that there had to be another way in.

I got dressed as quick as I could and headed for the university library. After a full hour I had discovered a huge number of books on gold mines and mining. But nothing I could use right off. So I did the next most logical thing. I headed over to the College of Mines. It was supposed to be the best in the country, so it seemed realistic that someone there would be able to answer my question.

And I was right. A mining grad student named Carol occupied the giant wooden front desk in the college office. She stood, on a good day, five foot even, and had big brown eyes and a smile that made me stammer. The desk dwarfed her, yet somehow she held her own against it.

She listened patiently to my request and then took me to a huge book of diagrams about how most gold mines were dug in the northwest, depending on location and ground formation.

I told her what the area around Grandpa's mine looked like, approximately when it was dug and told her it was in this area. She showed me how those mines would have been dug, made me copies of diagrams, and then asked if there was anything else she could help me with.

"Actually, there is," I said. "I was wondering if it was normal, and how, and maybe why, someone would open a second entrance to a mine."

"Sure. They did it like this," she said and flipped to a section farther back in the same volume. It took her a moment to find what she was looking for, then pointed it out to me. "Almost always they went sideways along the same line and started a new shaft. Usually the second shaft would angle in to help cut down distance to the surface after a main shaft had followed a vein too far underground."

I stared at the illustration. It seemed so simple in drawings, but I knew what that hillside looked like, covered in thick trees and brush. This was not going to be as easy as it sounded.

"Of course," Carol said, "if the original shaft went down or up following the vein, then they would start the second shaft to attempt to match the rise or fall."

I sighed. "What you are telling me is if there is a second shaft it could be anywhere in a radius of 500 feet around the first shaft."

Again she laughed. I was starting to enjoy that sound even though she was mostly laughing at my problem. "Actually it could be a lot farther than five hundred feet. Some of the old gold mines in this area went on for thousands of feet underground."

"Great. Just great. You want to spend some time with me Saturday hiking in the mountains looking for a mine?" I actually meant the question almost jokingly.

"I'd love to," she said, "on one condition."

"What's that?"

"You tell me your name."

I did and we also agreed to have dinner Friday evening. I left thanking Grandpa and his stupid mine. The week was looking up.

FIVE

Moscow, Idaho
October 21, 2035

THIS WOULD BE my last trip into the dead city. It seemed sort of obvious that I should make this trip on the anniversary of the date Carol and I found the second entrance to the mine.

I plan on leaving the government van just inside the edge of what is not so laughingly called the Dead Zone and walk the rest of the way. I should be able to cover my tracks enough that it will never occur to anyone to trace me to my parents' old home. Besides, as long as they get the van back, no one is going to waste much time on an old man like me. Not after all these years.

Carol would have laughed at this as being stupid. But Carol died of cancer years ago. I always blamed the mountain for her death. I suppose now it is responsible for mine. But I am old and don't have much time left anyway. If she were still alive she would have known where I would have gone. She would have tried to stop me. But she is no longer with me. Has not been for years. Now I would rather just be left alone.

I think she would have understood that.

I park the van near the road beside what had been an old gas station. The bright yellow of the van stands out against the dull gray of the dust. They will have no problem finding it.

I leave tracks into the gas station and then out the other side, letting my prints blend into others I have made over the years. Then I move out onto the road and start walking toward town, staying within the tracks the van has left during my hundreds of visits. My footprints will never show.

I walk slow, taking my time. I am old and the hills around this little city are steep. Besides, I am in no hurry.

SIX

Boise, Idaho
August 16, 1913

HAROLD GILET STOOD against the back wall of the hot courtroom and watched Clarence Darrow stride back and forth in front of the jury of twelve men, all dressed in suits, all looking very uncomfortable in the heat. Hundreds of reporters and spectators jammed the room, their notepads held at ready, some scratching down what Darrow was saying, others using the pads as fans.

The huge open windows of the courthouse let in the street noise and once in a while a breath of breeze, but not near enough to suit Harold. He used today's newspaper to fan himself, but even that didn't seem to help. The heat and the smell of packed human flesh was overwhelming.

But he couldn't leave. He had to stay to get his suspicions confirmed one way or another. The Governor had been killed because of a gold mine outside of Moscow, not because of the union problems in the silver mines farther north.

But as yet, in all the days of the trial, not one word of the old gold mine had

been spoken. It was as if no one knew about it.

Senator Borah, the Boy Orator as they called him in Washington D.C., sat peacefully at a table in front of the judge with Idaho State's Attorney General. Harold could tell that the Senator was listening intently to every word Darrow said. Darrow was considered the hottest young attorney in the nation. When he had offered to defend John Stevens for free in the bombing death of the Governor, the Attorney General had called Washington and asked if Senator Borah would come home and help in the prosecution for the state.

Of course the case had brought the press. Besides having a Governor assassinated, the future of the unions in the silver mines of Northern Idaho rode on this trial. And the future of a lot of mining unions all over the country.

If Stevens could be proven to have union connections and the Governor was killed on the orders of the unions as everyone suspected, the mine's owners would win. The unions would be dead. But if Stevens was just a lone wolf, taking his hatred of the mines, and what they had done to him and his family, out on the Governor, then that would not hurt the unions. And the fighting would continue.

But Harold Gilet was sure the Governor's death was because of another mine completely. A lost gold mine outside of the northern town of Moscow. He had overheard the wildest conversation possible two days before the Governor was killed.

He had been up in Idaho City, courting Mary, his soon to be wife. Her dad had a small placer claim there and had built Mary and her mother a cabin just above the creek. Harold had camped down and across the creek in a small grove of pine trees. Somewhere in the early morning hours he woke to the sound of a horse just beyond the grove. His fire had died down to nothing more than embers and through the trees he could see the faint flickering of a light.

With gun in one hand, he crept from his bedroll and moved silently toward the light. Beside the creek trail a man stood, holding the reins of a horse with one hand and a small lantern with the other. He seemed to be staring off down the trail in the direction of Idaho City.

So Harold settled in and waited. In this part of the country, unless you wanted to be shot, you never sneaked up on another man. Too many claim jumpers still working the mountains.

In a very short time another rider approached and dismounted. He was wearing the clothes of a gentleman even at this time of the night. Harold could even see the chain of the man's pocket watch hanging from his vest. He was obviously from Idaho City or Boise.

"You got the caps?" the gentleman asked the other, who was dressed like a dirt miner and wore a rain slicker, even though it wasn't raining. Harold now wished he had gotten closer because he couldn't see either of their faces in the flickering lantern light.

The miner patted the horse's saddle bags. "All set. I'll pick up the dynamite down on the river."

"Good," the gentleman said. "Make sure you make it look right. Then get back north to Moscow."

"Don't you worry. The union will take the fall. You sure about this?"

Harold could see the gentleman nod. "Absolutely. We can't let word of the gold mine get out. Outside of Moscow he's the only one who knows about it. It was a mistake to tell him about it. With him gone and the mine on the back side of that mountain, no one is going to find it. Better that it stays lost."

Without a handshake or another word both men mounted up and rode off in different directions. Harold went back to be wondering what that had been all about. The next day Mary agreed to be his wife and two days later he heard about the Governor being killed by a bomb.

He and Mary were married in Idaho City and then moved down to Boise When the trial started, Harold crowded into the courtroom every day with the reporters. He had thought about going to the Attorney General with what he had heard, but he couldn't identify the men and the more he thought about it the more none of what he had heard made sense. He decided to wait and see if anything about a lost gold mine came up in the trial. If it did he would then tell what he had heard.

But not one word was ever said about a lost gold mine outside of Moscow. Stevens was convicted, without a connection made between him and the unions. Over the next year Harold couldn't seem to shake the idea of there being a lost gold mine outside of Moscow. A mine that had gotten the Governor of the state killed.

So with the help of Mary's father, the following summer they moved to Moscow with the idea that Harold would get an engineering degree. That summer Harold helped with the wheat harvest around Moscow and that fall he started school at the new land grant university there.

On weekends, without telling anyone, he explored the back side of Moscow Mountain.

SEVEN

Moscow, Idaho
October 21, 1999

CAROL ENDED UP knowing a great deal more about mountain hiking than I did. She discovered that fact over dinner Friday and later at her apartment. I didn't much care. By Saturday morning I was in love with the short, brown-haired grad student. She could lead me into any wilderness area she wanted, any time she wanted.

But where she did lead me first thing Saturday morning was to the local outdoor supply store. She had me buy a good pair of boots and a thick pair of gloves. We picked up a pack, a small ax and a folding shovel. Also three flashlights and a good lantern, just in case. By the time we added food, matches, and toilet paper, I was out two hundred bucks.

We left my car at my Grandfather's place where Dad joined us. After I introduced him to Carol he whistled at my new boots and gloves and nodded thoughtfully at the sight of the shovel, ax, and flashlights. I had told Dad the day before what we were planning on looking for and when. He had gotten really excited and decided to join us. At first I had been annoyed at that. I had hoped to spend the time alone with Carol. But after spending the night with her, it now didn't matter. I just knew we were going to be spending a lot of time together for years to come.

Dad had packed us a large knapsack of lunch and when we reached the mine sight he dropped the sack on a stump and sat down beside it. I could tell he was breathing hard, but I couldn't tell if it was from the climb or the excitement. Carol was fine, not even winded. I thought I was in good shape from football, but that climb had still made me suck a little air. Carol just kept on impressing me.

Carol dropped her small pack and moved over in front of the old mine entrance. She climbed in around the bushes, studying the old entrance to the mine and then the rocks around it. "Looks to me," she said, pointing at the angle of the rock outcropping, "that they followed the vein in here and went down at a slight angle and to the right."

"So we look down there?" I asked, pointing in the direction of the old road.

She shrugged. "Seems as logical as any place to start. Remember, chances are it won't look like a mine entrance. And it might go straight down to start and then turn inward."

"So what exactly should we look for?" Dad said.

Again Carol shrugged. "Anything that looks odd. Maybe nothing more than a slight depression in the side of the hill."

"Simple enough," I said.

Carol only laughed.

Of course, she was right. It turned out anything but simple. We spread out and slowly angled our way down the hill to the right of the mine, climbing over logs, slipping on loose sticks, scratching our faces and arms on sharp brush.

Two hours and two breaks later it was Dad who finally spotted the entrance.

"Gary. Carol. Over here," he called out and I scrambled up through some thick brush to reach his side just as Carol came down through the trees above him.

At first I couldn't see what he was looking at. But then slowly it became clear. Behind some branches and slightly to the side of a huge pine there were some old wooden planks covered with dirt and rock. Actually the only reason he had even found it was that a deer had used the area to bed down and had knocked off some of the layers of rock, dirt, and pine needles, uncovering one of the boards.

"Wow," Carol said, studying the old board and the area around it. "Someone really didn't want this found, did they?"

"Sure seems that way," Dad said. "Actually, the more I read the old journal, the more I think this place was something much more than a gold mine."

"Well," I said. "Let's open it up and find out, shall we? Carol, any suggestions as to how we might go about this?"

"Carefully, would be my suggestion. Very carefully. These old mines can be very dangerous. Wood exposed to the elements for seventy or eighty years will be completely rotten."

We spent the next hour slowly opening up the hole. The one thing we hadn't remembered to bring was a hammer, so the shovel and ax served for most of the duty.

The second entrance turned out to be a hole about five feet square that went straight down into the ground about ten feet. An old wooden ladder was secured against one wall. The shaft of the mine turned directly into the hillside. Obviously this entrance had been built to be covered easily and hidden. Carol said she was impressed that there were no signs at all of tailings. She said they must have hauled all the dirt out by bucket and then by wheelbarrow.

It was two in the afternoon before we finally had the entrance cleared enough to go in. Carol was getting as excited as Dad and I. It was fun watching her and her radiant smile as she worked at cleaning back the brush and old wood.

Dad had brought a short rope with him, so we tied it to the closest pine and tossed it down into the hole. "Chance are the old ladder is rotted. But we might as will try to use it. Just keep hold of the rope."

"Let me try first," Carol said, "since I'm the smallest."

Dad nodded and Carol dropped on her stomach and then slowly inched her way over the lip of the hole and down. The ladder held her and the floor of the hole was solid dirt. I didn't bother with the ladder. I just lowered myself over the edge and dropped to the bottom. Then with Carol on one side and me on the other we helped Dad down the old ladder.

"Lights," Dad said, clicking on his light and ducking inside the old tunnel.

"Not too fast," Carol said. "Let me check out the timbers. We don't want this caving in on us."

Dad stopped and Carol eased around him, shining her flashlight on the beams and old support timbers. It was clear to even my eye that whoever had built this had made it to last.

Not one ounce of dirt was in sight. The ceiling, walls, and floors were all covered completely by wood after a few feet inside the entrance. Carol could stand up straight in the tunnel, but both Dad and I had to duck.

"Wow!" Carol said. "I've never seen anything like this. No reason to build all this unless you planned on living in here."

"This place gets stranger and stranger," I said.

Dad agreed and pointed his light down the tunnel. It curved to the left about twenty feet ahead. With Carol in the lead we worked our way underground along the wooden corridor, Carol walking slowly and cautiously, testing each step. Dad and I bent over, following her.

We must have gone a good hundred yards, with two turns and a slight downward angle before we hit another tunnel.

"Main tunnel," Carol said. She pointed her light back up the incline. "This heads right in the direction of the meadow."

In the main tunnel I could stand up completely without even coming close to the high ceiling and my back was very glad that I could. But on top of the back ache I was starting to get a real uneasy feeling about this place. The main tunnel was also completely enclosed by wood and every twenty feet there was an old lantern hanging on a peg from a support beam. Someone had spent a huge amount of time and money in here. And not recently. I shined my light around the wider main tunnel.

"Carol, any reason they would shore this up like this?"

"Not if this was a regular gold mine. No." She shined her light at the wood planks of the floor. "No rails or any other way to get the gold ore out of here. And there is no reason to have a gold mine shaft this wide and big. My guess is that if this was a gold mine, then it was expanded and the flooring and walls were put in after the mining was finished."

"Why would anyone do that?" Dad asked.

Carol shrugged. "Never heard of it before," she said. "But I imagine the answer is down there." She pointed the flashlight down the tunnel. "Maybe someone really did live here."

"You as creeped out by this place as I am?" I asked.

Both Dad and Carol nodded. Then Carol led the way, again going slow and cautious.

About two hundred feet later we found the answer to our question. The mine shaft ran smack into a solid metal wall. The tunnel branched both left and right, following the curve of the metal off in both directions.

"What the hell is this?" Dad said, rubbing his hand along the metal. "It's manufactured. Why...?"

Carol and I both were running our hands along the smooth gray metal. It felt cold and polished to my touch, like the hood of a car. And the curve into the distance in both directions was exact, with no markings or anything else. "Carol?" I asked, "How far underground would you think we are?"

Carol kept running her hand over the surface of the metal, as if not really believing that it was there. I didn't believe it either. After a moment she looked over at me and pointed upward. "In that direction I would say a good thousand plus feet." She pointed at an angle back along the main tunnel. "In that direction more like five hundred."

I looked off in both directions. "Why would someone build this down here? And for what reason?"

Carol walked a few feet to the right, running her hand along the metal. "You might want to consider that they found this here while digging for gold."

Dad turned and walked away from the metal, back up the tunnel, then turned around and sat down on the wood planking, facing the metal wall. "Not possible," he said. "That would make this, whatever it is, over a million years old. These are young mountains around here, but not that young."

Carol nodded. "At this depth it would be at least that old. Maybe much more."

We stood there in silence, our flashlight beams glued to the metal surface. My mind was just not accepting what I was seeing. None of this could be true. None of it. My Grandpa had been a crazy old man. And in the later years his laugh had driven me nuts. For some reason he

had built this down here and all we had to do was keep exploring until we found out why. "Dad, let's keep going." I pointed to the right. "Might be some answers."

Dad nodded slowly and climbed back to his feet. This time I led the way. Not a seam in the metal, nothing, as we slowly curved down and to the left. For a short time I thought we were just going to end up circling around and ending back up at the junction of the main tunnel.

But then I found the open airlock.

And there was no longer any doubt as to what we had found.

No wonder Grandpa had joined the Lost Wheelbarrow Mine Association to keep the mine hidden. This discovery would blow the lid off of the current world, let alone the world of 1915. Of that there was no doubt.

EIGHT

Moscow, Idaho
October 21, 2035

I CAREFULLY PLACED my boots in the exact same footprints as I always had as I started down the street. Nothing had changed in the months since I had been here. Of course, it never did. This street was frozen in time, locked in death by my family's stupidity.

The gray dust made no noise through my protective suit and in front of my parents' house I stopped and looked around. I could imagine the times when we used to play football in that street. I could remember the laughter and the fun. I had always played receiver, so I got to duck in and out of the parked cars, trying to get free to catch the pass. I usually did. I was always good at football.

Those summer and fall days were full of cut grass smells and the tastes of carnivals. Life back then seemed to have no problems and no worries. Now I had finally returned to that point. It is lucky that Carol has been dead all these years. She would call me self pitying. She would be right.

My parents and everyone in Moscow and the surrounding area were killed when Dad's team tried to start up the simplest power system in the buried ship. Now no children would ever play in these streets again.

I stood on my parents' front steps and tried to remember the laughter.

NINE

Berkeley, California
July10, 2015.

I STOOD IN front of the television, my mouth open, staring.

"Over a hundred square miles," the CNN announcer said, "of Northern Idaho has been evacuated. The gray cloud causing the deaths has slowly settled over the Moscow, Idaho, area. No reason for the cloud has been uncovered, but the theory that a small mountain to the north of Moscow has erupted is not true. We will keep you updated as more information comes in."

"Dad? Mom?" Carol put her arm around me, holding me while crying. I couldn't cry. I was too much in shock.

I just kept staring at the television, not really believing what I knew must have happened.

The day we found the buried spaceship Carol and I and Dad had sat inside the control room in the alien chairs. Just as Grandpa and the men before him, we decided that the world wasn't ready for this discovery. We decided that Grandpa and the old Wheelbarrow Association had been right. This ship needed to stay secret for a while. Or at the very least bring outsiders in slowly.

Dad had taken charge and within a week had brought in a trusted friend who was a professor of physics at Cal Tech. Then over the next few years the Wheelbarrow Association, as we called ourselves, gained more and more members as Dad put together a private research team made up of some of the best scientists in the nation to study the ship.

They made slow headway, filing patents on what they did figure out how to work, and being careful to document every step they took.

Carol and I were married the following year and both of us kept going to school and working around the ship in the summers. After a few years we even came to feel comfortable with knowing there was an alien ship buried under Moscow Mountain. It became a part of our lives. I took a job at the University of California, Berkeley, doing research in electrical engineering, mostly along lines we were uncovering in the ship. Carol finished her doctorate in geology and was teaching across the bay.

We spent the summers in Moscow.

Life for all of us was good. Settled. Until the research team decided to start one of the ship's power systems. For years nothing that crazy had been suggested. That summer I spent time on the ship arguing against trying to power anything up. I argued that the systems the aliens were using were not completely understood yet. I argued that there was a real reason this ship was here that we didn't understand and that reason might have to do with a malfunction in the power systems. We didn't know what might happen.

But Dad and his team said it was right to try, all safety precautions would be taken, and everything would be done by the book.

Dad and his friends didn't say what book.

I helped with the early stages, hoping against hope that I could talk them out of trying anything. But all the research and all the exacting detailed studies went so smoothly that eventually, when school started, Carol and I went back to California.

Every night I talked to Dad and some of the other scientists. And three times that fall I went back up to try to stop the testing. But I had no luck. From what Dad told me on the phone the night before they were all killed, everything still seemed just fine. Powering up the smallest power system seemed to be progressing as planned and he was excited about finally getting into some of the data banks on the ship. I was supposed to call him and be on the phone when the test started in case they needed me for anything.

But, of course, something went wrong. Terribly wrong.

Carol and I were eating breakfast when we heard the news of what they were calling an explosion in Northern Idaho during the night. I had been expecting a call from Dad about the test being postponed for one reason or another. I was sure there would be small problems that would stop the power-up for a few more weeks. But I guess I was wrong.

At first the news sources thought that Moscow Mountain had blown itself apart in a volcanic eruption sometime around three in the morning. But Moscow Mountain was still there and could be photographed from a distance. And there had been no seismic activity that night to show an explosion.

Carol and I knew what had happened. The ship had gone through a meltdown of some sort or another. The test Dad and the rest had wanted to try had not been scheduled to start until later in the morning. Dad was still in bed, at home, with Mom, when the accident occurred.

After staring at the news reports for most of the morning, I finally stood and went to the phone.

Carol moved up beside me and touched my shoulder lightly as I dialed the phone to finally tell the world about the alien spaceship in the Lost Wheelbarrow Mine.

Of course, at that point it was way too late.

TEN

Moscow, Idaho
October 21, 2035

I LOOKED DOWN the gray-coated street. Maybe the ghosts of all the dead children were still playing there. Maybe after today I would be able to see them, hear their laughter. It would be nice to see laughter on this street again.

The gray dust under my feet was the same color as I remembered the hull of the ship. A vast cloud of gray dust, probably material from the hull, had poured out of the northern side of the mountain.

In the end it was lucky that there was very little wind. The cloud of gray dust settled silently in the night over the small city of Moscow, Idaho, and killed everyone in that city instantly. Most in their sleep.

The specialists say that if there had been a wind it could have been much worse, taking out Missoula and other cities east.

By the next morning the dust had quit spewing from the side of the mountain and it rained. A simple fall rain that turned the gray dust into something harder than concrete, gluing death to everything it touched.

Exploration teams eventually entered the mountain and the old mine and found what was left, a melted mass of grayness in a huge empty hole in the ground. They explored that hole for a while, until it became clear there was nothing to gain. Then they left and sealed off the area. Left the dead frozen in their sleep. Set up guards to keep the world out.

There was nothing else the world could do.

No one lives within a hundred-mile radius of Moscow, Idaho, now.

And no one will for centuries.

I took one last look at the street, hoping to see children playing there. Then I turned into the house. Carefully placing my feet in my footprints from my very first visit I climbed the stairs to my parents' room.

For only a moment I thought about going down to my old room, to the safety it offered. But then turned and went into their room.

"Hi, Mom. Hi, Dad," I said, but my voice echoed around inside my protective suit. "I'd like to pretend it's Christmas morning. Can I join you?"

Without waiting for an answer I strode across the unmarked dust on the floor around their bed.

I unzipped my suit, took off my helmet, and took a deep breath. The air smelled dry and stale and I felt my eyelids getting heavy.

Quickly I jumped onto the bed and then laid down beside Mom. I didn't look at them because I didn't want to know if I had disturbed the scene.

I took another deep breath and let it slowly out. For a moment I thought I could smell Grandpa's pipe smoke and hear his cackling, crazy laughter.

For some reason that made me smile.

I took one last deep breath.

Outside, beyond the window, I heard the sounds of children laughing and playing in the street.

~

Now Available
from all your favorite booksellers
in trade paper and electronic editions.

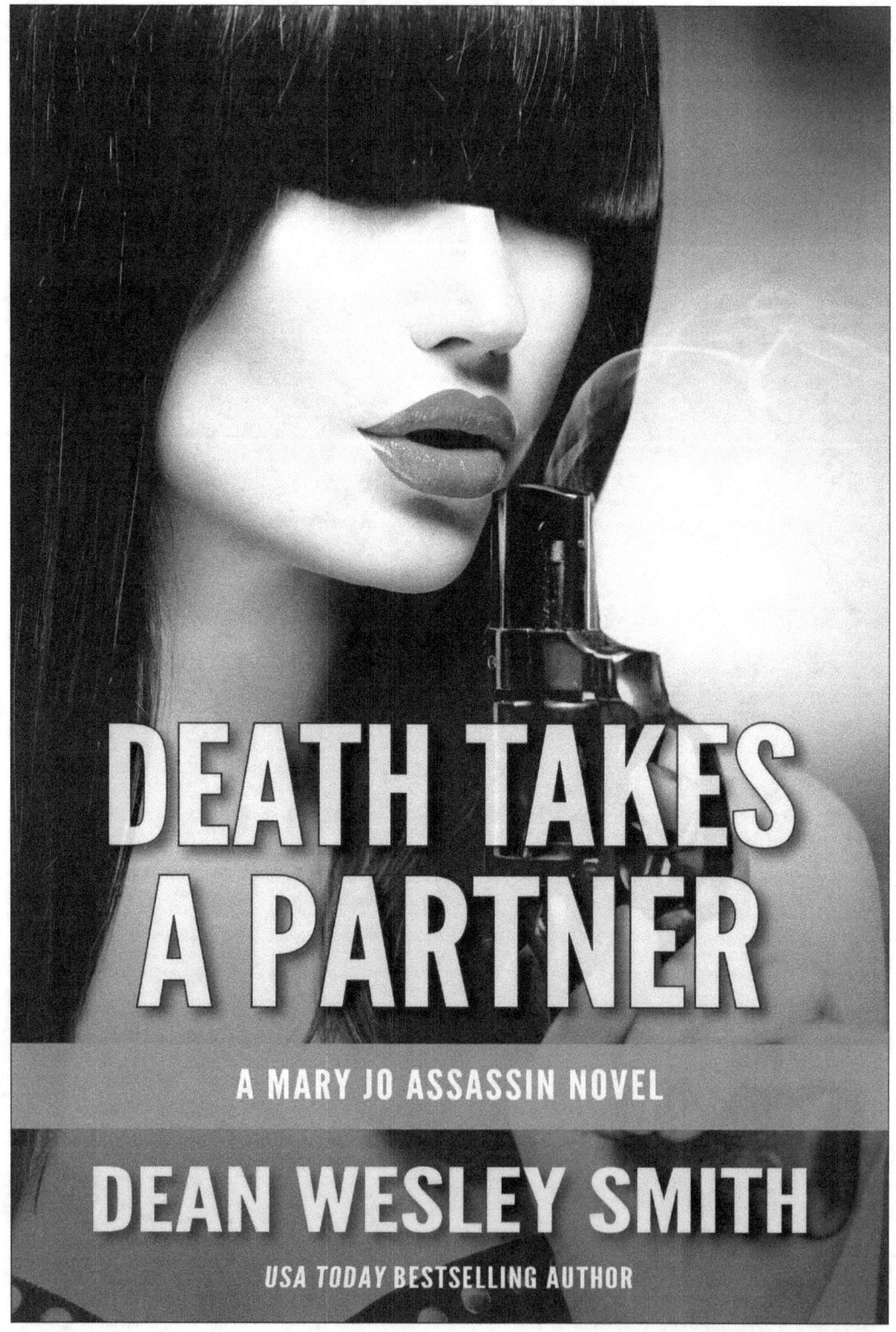

DEATH TAKES A PARTNER

A MARY JO ASSASSIN NOVEL

DEAN WESLEY SMITH

USA TODAY BESTSELLING AUTHOR

Mary Jo, one of the most beautiful and deadly assassins in all history, loves drinking vodka and orange juice after a job well done.

She planned her next kill perfectly. Every detail thought through.

But Mary Jo never planned on meeting Jean, the beautiful woman two houses down the street.

Jean also loves drinking vodka and orange juice after a job well done.

A twisted story of love, killing, and drinking, not necessarily in that order.

DEATH TAKES A PARTNER
A Mary Jo Assassin Novel

PART ONE
The Stage is Set

CHAPTER ONE

MARY JO STOOD in her kitchen, staring at the bottle of Smirnoff Vodka in her hand. Actually, it only said Smirnoff on the outside. She had poured out the Smirnoff and replaced it with Absolut Crystal, one of the more expensive vodkas in the world. But she had to keep the fact that she could easily afford Absolut Crystal hidden.

She had a pitcher of orange juice beside her on the counter, ice was a touch away in the fridge, and a highball glass sat waiting.

That wonderful taste of fresh orange juice over ice with the slight flavor of a very good vodka could make a girl smile and she liked to smile.

She made herself look away from the bottle of vodka like a lover turning from a night of sex with a great date.

She was fairly certain she could have just one more. But she needed to be sure. Not like the day-after pill sure, but full condom and birth-control pills sure.

She thought she had done everything right. But she needed to check it all again.

The gray granite counter surface was spotless, the white cabinets wiped down completely, the dark tile floor scrubbed.

Not a spot of blood could have survived in this modern suburban kitchen. She had even opened every cabinet door and made sure nothing had dripped down onto a hinge or in a crack. She had sanitized every tiny inch with bleach.

Sometimes more than once just to be sure.

She had come to love the smell of bleach over the years. It always signaled a job well done in her mind, which then led her to top-shelf vodka mixed with fresh orange juice.

She had put nothing down any sink, but instead used a plastic bucket for the cleaning water. Then outside in the fenced back yard she had washed the bucket out completely in the gravel at the back end of the path to the yard.

Then she had put the bucket in the ground in a new flowerbed full of roses that she had planted last week. She had punched some holes in the bottom of the bucket, put a new ground-cover plant in the bucket, and filled the bucket up with dirt.

The bucket was covered completely.

It was gone.

Then she had turned on the sprinklers that watered the lawn, including the area of the path where she had poured the cleaning water.

She was very good at this sort of thing. Very, very good.

At five-one and a pixie-like body, no one would ever suspect her abilities to kill. For centuries, her looks had always given her an advantage. And she had used the advantage often.

Now, as a modern housewife living on a suburban street in a small town in upstate New York, the idea that she might be able to kill would be ludicrous to anyone who had met her.

A deadly misjudgment on some people's part.

She stared at the bottle of vodka and the pitcher of orange juice. It had been a perfect day so far.

She could have just one more, she was sure.

But instead she stood there, thinking back over the events so far, the drink not yet poured.

Mary Jo had to make double and triple sure.

Safety first in both sex and murder.

CHAPTER TWO

Three Hours Earlier

JEAN FINISHED THE last project for the afternoon and sat back in her oversized (for her) office chair. At five-three and with a tiny stature, no office chair had ever fit her. She had used pillows at times to support her back and a footrest for her feet, but those pillows, at the moment, were on the hardwood oak floor in her office, near her couch.

She had one of the best offices in all of Benton with a view of the surrounding rolling pine-covered hills and the river that cut along the side of the small city.

She turned and just let the peaceful view relax her. It would only be a little longer before her mission here was complete. It might be another six months before she could really move on, but that didn't matter. She had the patience that came with living for thousands of years.

The patience of a hunter.

And she was one of the best hunters and killers there was.

She glanced around. She might actually miss this office. She didn't need the job or the money, but her husband Sam didn't know that. And besides, she found this modern job challenging and the people here in the office were friendly. They all fell totally for her role, and her story about working to let her husband stay home and write novels.

Her husband Sam was a nice guy. Gentle and friendly and always willing to help. Not that good a writer, but decent enough to maybe have a chance of selling someday. Too bad he wasn't going to live long enough for that to happen.

He was just her cover to get to her real target and when she finished off her real target, she wouldn't be able to leave any loose ends, no matter how much she liked him.

Too bad she didn't love him. If she had, she might have worked to find a different way. Sadly, she hadn't fallen in love with anyone for a very long time.

And that thought just depressed her.

She stood to get her pillows and put them behind her back again as she started on a new project.

The work at least kept her mind busy until she could get to her real job and kill her target.

That would be soon.

Very soon.

CHAPTER THREE

Three Hours Earlier

MARY JO SMILED as her neighbor Sam stood on the ladder in her hall and finished fixing the light that had been shorting on and off. Mary Jo had caused the short and then asked Sam, the friendly writer from three houses down the street, to help her fix it before it burnt down her house.

An easy excuse in the middle of the afternoon that no good neighbor could refuse.

Sam was one of the nicest men Mary Jo had ever met. Maybe in his late thirties, balding with only thin brown hair and a grin that reminded her of a nice puppy wanting to be petted. She had only seen his wife from a distance. She was an attractive small woman and they looked to be a happy couple. Mary Jo knew that Sam's wife worked downtown somewhere so that he could stay home and write a novel.

How cliché as far as Mary Jo was concerned.

But perfect for what Mary Jo needed at the moment.

"Got it," Sam said, pride at his own small accomplishment in his voice.

She clicked on the light and the bulb burnt steady.

"Wonderful," she said, smiling as Sam climbed down and folded up the ladder.

"That calls for a quick drink," Mary Jo said. "I owe you. You like screwdrivers?"

Sam beamed, the smile reaching his brown eyes. "Love them. And so does my wife. I think at times she might be able to live on them."

"Well, this one is on me," Mary Jo said, watching as Sam put the ladder away and noting carefully what he touched and exactly where. She would clean off his prints later, including inside the light fixture.

Then she led the way into the modern, bright kitchen with its stainless steel appliances, white cabinets and granite countertops. The floor was covered in a dark tile that contrasted perfectly with the cabinets. All the houses in this neighborhood had modern kitchens like this one.

"Make mine a small one," Sam said. "Still got to finish that chapter."

"No problem," Mary Jo said.

She took down the bottle that said Smirnoff on the outside and two glasses.

"Ice in the fridge," she said.

As Sam turned to get the ice, she drove a long ice pick through his back and directly into his heart. He was on the floor almost instantly, bleeding only slightly.

He had a puzzled look in his brown eyes.

"Sorry," Mary Jo said to Sam as the light in his eyes faded. "Just needed a body and yours was handy. If you wrote mystery novels, I'm sure you would understand."

Sam took one last breath and died.

Mary Jo got the ice from the fridge, put Sam's glass in the sink to wash in a minute, filled her glass, then added vodka and orange juice. She had her first drink of the day watching Sam slowly bleed onto her kitchen tile floor.

Drink tasted damn good.

She loved screwdrivers.

CHAPTER FOUR

JEAN PUSHED BACK and stood, glancing at her watch.

Almost three in the afternoon.

She had a routine at this time of the day because her target had a routine as well.

Her target was the Chief of Police for Benton, Robert Hanson. It seemed he had really, really made someone with a lot of money very, very angry. So this someone had hired her to take care of the chief.

One million up front, two million on completion of the job.

She had made it clear to the man who hired her that it would take her almost a year to kill the target. She liked working slowly and carefully.

The guy didn't care, just wanted it done.

So she had met dear old Sam, they had moved to Benton and she had taken a job so he could write, and three months later they had gotten married. In her long life, she couldn't remember how many times she had been married.

And then widowed.

Or even under how many names.

The wedding with Sam had just been another of the small and completely forgettable ones, with only his family and friends, since she had told him her family was dead. That was a truth. Her original family had been dead for a couple thousand years, all killed right after they sold her as a young woman to the order of assassins.

She headed down to the street level. The day was a nice fall day, with a slight wind from the west. She didn't need a jacket, but in just a few weeks the leaves on the trees would change and the snow would arrive soon after.

Fall here in this part of New York State was pretty, but she had no interest in staying through another winter, even though she knew she would have to, just to make sure no suspicion fell on her.

Two blocks down from her office was a wonderful bakery called Ben's. He had the best cinnamon rolls and actually a decent cup of coffee.

Chief Hanson sat in his normal spot near the front window, talking and laughing with two of the town's citizens.

It seemed from what Jean had heard around town that Chief Hanson liked to be open to people coming and talking with him if he wasn't busy on call. And he held those meetings in the main window of Ben's Bakery.

Jean smiled as she went in to get herself a bagel with cream cheese and some hot tea. She loved the rich, thick freshbread smell of the bakery, mixed only slightly with the sweet odor of fresh pastries. Ben's was one of those old-fashioned bakeries you didn't see too often, with a dozen wooden tables and five huge antique display cabinets with the fresh cookies, pies, cakes and breads of the day.

She was going to miss this bakery more than anything about this small town.

She took her bagel and tea to go and went back into the crisp fall air. Across the river was a small rise of trees that gave clear line-of-sight to the front window where the chief always sat. She had considered killing him that way, since she was an expert sniper, but decided that it didn't leave her a clean getaway.

So she had decided instead on a bomb, powerful, set to explode when he started his car. She could easily plant it on her break and be back in her office when the explosion occurred.

It would be too simple, actually. She had been surprised that the chief always parked his car in the exact same spot every day, secluded from sight of windows or cameras, tucked off to the west of the police station.

Clearly the chief didn't realize that he had made someone very rich very angry.

It had taken her about a month, once she had decided on the plan, to carefully round up the ingredients needed for the bomb. Only the explosives had been a problem and she had killed the man who had delivered them just to make sure there were no connections to her.

That guy's body would never be found. She had buried him four feet down in the woods fifty miles to the north and covered his body with a quick-acting acid. That had been three weeks ago and by now there would be nothing but a sticky mess left of that guy.

As she turned on the sidewalk to head back to work, the chief caught her eye and smiled. She smiled back and gave him a slight wave.

The chief was a friendly guy, of that there was no doubt.

And he would be worth three million to her dead.

And even though she didn't need the money, she liked that a great deal.

CHAPTER FIVE

MARY JO HAD used a wheelbarrow to get the plastic-wrapped body of Sam the writer out and into the back of her Jeep in her garage. That had been a struggle, but luckily she was a lot stronger than her small size would show.

She had only done a surface job of cleaning. When she got back she would take care of everything completely.

Once she had good old Sam in the back of the Jeep, she had covered him in what looked to be piles of full black bags of garbage. Actually, each sack was full of nothing more than foam used in stuffing pillows and stuffed animals. She had bought the foam months earlier with the excuse of stuffing some dolls for needy kids.

But they also stuffed black garbage bags perfectly as well to look like pretend garbage headed to the landfill.

She headed north out of town, driving right at the speed limit with the window down to let in the wonderful fresh afternoon air. Fall in New York State was always a wonderful time, even though the deep snow of the winter was right around the corner.

She liked it here. Not enough to stay longer than she would need to stay, but still, it had turned into a nice place to live.

She followed an old road off the main highway until she found the turnoff she was looking for.

She had paid a man ten thousand to steal a pickup truck from a neighboring state and leave it here. The man had never seen her and she had never seen him, which kept him alive.

As of yesterday afternoon, the dark brown Ford pickup was there, hidden behind some large brush.

Wearing skintight gloves that left false fingerprints, she moved the truck around to a position behind her Jeep and lowered the tailgate. Then she slid Sam's body into the back of the truck, making sure it was still tightly wrapped in the heavy plastic.

She moved her Jeep into the place the truck had been, out of sight, and locked it. Anyone trying to get into it without her keyed password would be killed instantly by an explosion that would leave very little left to pick up.

The drive back into town in the truck was the part that worried her the most.

She put on a long, blonde wig and a skintight face mask that gave her wide cheeks and a pointed nose.

She put on a coat with padding that made her look much larger and a pair of dark-rimmed glasses.

Even with all that, if she got stopped by the police for anything, she would have to kill the cop and abandon her plan and she hated doing that now that she was so close.

Twenty minutes later she pulled the truck into a deserted rock quarry just outside of Benton. Checking the instruments in her purse to make sure that she wasn't being recorded in any way, she waited for a moment before climbing out.

No one around and all clear.

The sun in the bottom of the high-walled old rock quarry felt much warmer. She listened for any sounds of a car coming in the gravel road to the quarry and when she heard none, she opened the back tailgate and pulled out Sam's body, letting it flop on the ground.

She quickly unrolled him, leaving him face-up in the sun.

Then she folded the plastic, tucked it on the passenger floor of the truck, and quickly left.

Twenty-five minutes later she had the truck back hidden in the brush and her Jeep pointed down the road.

She took off her disguise and jacket she had worn and the thin gloves that left fake fingerprints and put them all on top of the plastic on the passenger side.

Then she took a bottle of quick-acting acid from her purse and covered the pile, watching the acid melt into the fabric and plastic.

She then lit a rag on fire and tossed it into the cab of the truck.

Using another rag to close the door, she moved around to the back of the truck, took off the gas cap and dropped two capsules into the tank.

Then she turned for her Jeep.

As she buckled into her seat, she heard a solid "thump" sound as the gas tank ignited.

As she pulled away, the truck was engulfed in flames and sadly, in short order, there would be a small forest fire going.

And a torched stolen truck would be to blame.

CHAPTER SIX

JEAN FOUND IT odd that Sam wasn't answering his cell phone. He always, with a frightening punctuality, called her at four every afternoon to see how she was doing and when she would be home.

Since Sam had agreed to stay home to write, he had decided he was going to cook for them as well. Bless his heart, he tried and sometimes his limited menu was pretty good.

Jean didn't actually mind cooking. But to make him feel better, she had agreed. Still, she had convinced him that three times a week they deserved to go out to eat. He needed to get out of the house besides just going to the grocery store for food and the hardware store for things to fix up the house.

She stared out her window at the wonderful, warm afternoon and the beautiful small city below as the phone rang.

And with each ring she got a little more worried. He had missed his normal call a few times before, but not often enough to be a habit, so this was strange.

Tonight she was looking forward to dinner and then a long soak in their hot tub.

She had to admit, what Sam lacked in abilities to cook, he made up for in construction skills. He had done a pretty nice job on adding in some nice features in the house, not the least of which was the wonderful hot tub on their back deck.

He had built a privacy barrier between the tub and the only neighbors who could see their deck, which allowed them to sit naked in the tub and just stare at the stars. On clear nights, the stars just seemed to really fill the sky. That was yet another advantage of living in a small town away from large cities.

The stars reminded her of simpler times thousands of years earlier. She would never want to go back to those times, but killing back then had sure been a much easier task.

Sam's phone finally went to voice mail and she listened to his upbeat voice telling her to leave a message.

"Give me a call when you come up from the chapter you are writing," she said and hung up.

Something didn't feel right, but she had no idea what that something might be. But over the centuries she had learned to trust that gut feeling.

So from this moment forward, she would be extra careful. Chances are it was just Sam being an airhead.

But she had her share of enemies as well, and there was no telling when one of them would come after her.

She would have no idea how anyone would have found her, but safe was better than sorry and very dead.

And since she had lived thousands of years now, she knew how to be safe.

CHAPTER SEVEN

MARY JO NEVER expected anything to lead back to her and her home, but it made no sense to take any chance when just a little bit of work would solve any problem.

After she had gotten back, she had removed all the black bags from the back of the Jeep and put them where they belonged, then had gone into the guest room, put her blouse, bra, underwear, jeans, shoes and socks in a black trash bag along with all the cloths she had used for the cleaning and set the bag near the back door.

Then she had gone to her own bedroom upstairs in the four-bedroom, two-bath suburban home, taken a shower, making sure she was clean.

Extra sure. Especially her short brown hair.

She had liked this house in the year since she and Bob had gotten married. It kind of fit a part of her that she didn't often get to enjoy. And she knew how to play the perfect housewife role to a science.

But behind the housewife, she was a member of an ancient order of assassins.

She had lived for thousands of years, as everyone in her order tended to do. And she had never grown tired of her job.

Not once. In fact, the job had gotten more and more challenging as technology improved.

She liked that and the money it supplied her to live a lavish lifestyle. She actually had no idea how rich she was, considering all of her many bank accounts around the world under all the different names. She actually didn't need to work, she just loved her job.

There was always a challenge. And she got to meet and sometimes marry nice people as well before killing them.

After her shower, she had dressed in a similar white blouse that she had had on earlier, same style of jeans, underwear, everything, including a second pair of identical sneakers.

With a pair of white gloves on, she took the black bag and put it into the back of her Jeep along with a couple bags of normal week's garbage. She had set this routine up a year ago. This was all normal for her, including the white gloves.

She had then driven the ten minutes to the landfill just outside of town, in the opposite direction from the rock quarry.

There she had made sure every bag was tossed over the edge of the dumping area into an area full of other black bags that a bulldozer was moving around and covering in layers of dirt.

She had paid the attendant in cash and he hadn't even noticed her other than to nod hi as he did every week. His attention was focused on the two pickup trucks behind her full of junk.

Now she was back at her house looking at the bottle of vodka and orange juice and wondering if she dared have just one more drink.

She loved her drinks, but was very careful in the thick of a job to not drink too much.

As she stood there, staring at the fixings for a drink she felt she wanted, but wasn't sure she needed, her cell phone went off.

It was her husband's ring.

She answered it. "Hi, honey."

"Afraid I'm going to be late for dinner," he said. "Got a body."

"Oh, no," she said, making herself take a deep breath.

Her husband was the Chief of Police for the entire city. This call was normal. Over their year of marriage it had happened a good thirty times.

She had been responsible for a few of those bodies, just as she was for dear old Sam, more than likely the one that had just been found. But he never knew that and never would.

Actually, she had been the one who had anonymously reported Sam's body from a burner phone she used while at the dump and then tucked into a black bag that went into the landfill. She didn't want to chance that no one would find her bait.

"I'm sorry to hear that," she said. "How about I wait for you and we go out to Murphy's Diner when you are done."

"Might get late," he said.

"I'll snack until you call."

"That would be nice," he said. He told her that he loved her and then hung up.

He was a good man.

She had enjoyed the year plus they had been together. The sex had been good, the laughter real. After centuries of living and killing, she had learned to appreciate those times even more.

She glanced at her watch. It was a quarter after five. The timing was spot on the money.

She glanced at the bottle of vodka one more time, then set it aside, put the pitcher of fresh orange juice back in the fridge and the clean glass back in the cabinet.

Maybe after her dinner.

She then took her purse and went out to her Jeep in the garage. The third row of seats were always down in her car so she could carry gardening and groceries easily.

She lifted the seat and there was the bag with a rifle in it. Also her disguise bag was there as well.

She slipped on her gloves for a moment and did a quick inventory to make sure everything was with the rifle and the disguise bag and she hadn't forgotten anything, then lowered the seats back into place.

Fifteen minutes later she had parked her Jeep in the mall parking lot out of any camera sight. She then, when no one was around, transferred her rifle to the small Ford four-door sedan back seat and locked the car. The car was brown, with plates mostly covered in mud.

The Ford sedan had been stolen by a man she had never met and left for her, just as another man had left the pickup for her. She had paid the man ten grand for the car in a drop bag. He hadn't asked questions.

Then, carrying her disguise bag, she went into the mall and into the public restroom as herself. She came out almost ten minutes later, after a half-dozen other women had come and gone, as a long-haired brunette with a much larger nose and a tan jacket and red tennis shoes.

She was ready to get this job done.

PART TWO
The Job

CHAPTER EIGHT

JEAN COULDN'T BELIEVE when she got home that Sam had vanished.

His cell phone was beside his computer, his car was in the garage, and the front door was unlocked.

His wallet and car keys were where he always left them in a dish in the entryway.

Jean quickly checked where they normally left notes for each other beside the fridge and there was nothing.

And no sign at all of any kind of scuffle.

She made herself do a complete check of the house. His clothes were still there, nothing had changed.

She went out into the backyard and walked the wooden fence-line, seeing if there was any sign anyone had come or gone that way.

Nothing.

She went back in and stood in the kitchen, looking around calmly.

Sam had simply walked out of the door.

Clearly for some reason.

But where was he? And why?

She needed to be prepared because if one of her enemies had found her, she needed to be ready.

But first she needed to find out what exactly had happened to Sam.

She went to their bedroom and pushed aside some of her clothes and clicked a tiny hidden switch on the back of the closet.

The switch tested her fingerprint to make sure it was her so that no one could accidently find what was behind the panel.

A very small section of the wall slid back and a computer screen and monitor slid forward.

She triggered the proximity alert around the house in case anyone approached. She wanted to be ready if they did.

Then she brought up the security system she had installed. Every inch of this house was recorded at all times. That would have driven Sam crazy if he would have known that, but she had lived a very long time by taking no chances.

Normally she would never check on Sam, but she had to know what had happened to him.

She fast-forwarded it to a time just slightly over three hours before. Sam had been working on his book when he suddenly turned.

He stood and went to the door and talked to a woman Jean knew from three doors down the street named Mary Jo Hanson.

The wife of Jean's target.

Mary Jo was an attractive and tiny woman with short brown hair.

Jean clicked on the sound and heard Mary Jo tell Sam that she had a light that

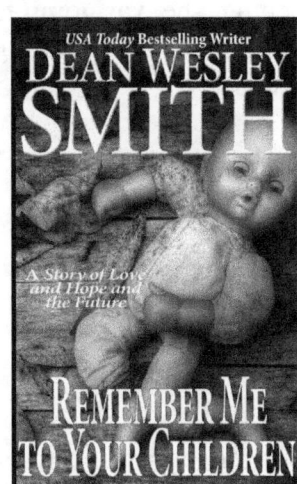

was shorting out in her hall and would he help her fix it.

He had agreed and from an external camera Jean watched Sam go down the sidewalk to Mary Jo's house and go in.

About thirty minutes later Mary Jo left her house in her Jeep, alone.

She came back almost an hour later, still alone.

She left once more for what must have been a short errand of some sort, then had left just ten minutes ago.

Jean was stunned. What was happening?

Was Sam still alive in there?

And what part had Sam played in whatever Mary Jo and her husband were up to?

She didn't dare go in there to look for him. All she could do at the moment was wait. Whatever was happening wasn't her doing.

She shut down her security panel, but not before extracting a pistol from a box inside the open wall. She made sure the clip was full and took a second clip.

Until she figured out exactly what was happening, she was going to stay armed.

And she was going to watch Mary Jo's house.

CHAPTER NINE

MARY JO WALKED from the mall to her stolen brown Ford sedan not drawing any attention to herself, climbed into the brown sedan and ten minutes later had it parked on the top of a pine-tree covered hill just to the right of town.

She had turned the car around so she could go straight down the hill she had just come up and be lost in the streets below in thirty seconds, long before anyone below even knew what hit them.

She left the car running and left the disguise bag in the car. She then took her rifle and made sure it was loaded.

It was actually a deer rifle, a classic bolt-action Roberts with a scope. The rifle was a collector's item that she remembered back sixty years ago really liking for a job similar to this one. The thief who had given her this rifle had assured her it was accurate and had been tested.

She tested it on him and he had been right, actually. The thief was still one of her husband's unsolved cases.

She moved to the small stone wall that kept tourists on this hill from tumbling over the edge of a fairly steep cliff down into an old stone quarry below. This small turn-around often held teens out parking for some first love experiences in a parent's car.

She was so old now, she could barely remember her first sexual experiences. They had not been pleasant, she remembered that much.

That's why she enjoyed the modern pleasant experiences now. Just like she enjoyed her drinks. When good, they were both worth savoring.

The rock quarry two hundred feet below was abandoned and mostly a playground for neighborhood kids after school and in the summer.

The body of good old Sam lay below her, right where she had dumped it. Someone had covered it.

Killing never did anything for her, one way or the other, and poor old Sam was just bait for her husband who was the real target.

She checked the area in the small clearing around her to make sure no one was nearby that she would also need to kill.

Thankfully it was clear.

Her husband stood with two detectives in a tight group near the body, talking.

Good, she would take care of all three at the same time. First her husband, who was her target, the one she was getting paid to kill. She had slept with her target for fourteen months. She thought of it like a cat playing with a mouse.

She studied the scene quickly one more time. By taking out the other two detectives, it would slow down any investigation.

"Goodbye, dear," she said softly. "This is what you get for pissing off the wrong people who have far too much money."

The rifle was loud, but had almost no kick.

The echo of her first shot bounced around through the trees and over the surrounding farmlands and down against the rock walls.

Her husband went to the ground instantly.

She knew the entry wound would be small in his chest, but most of his back would be blown away from the high-velocity rifle as the hollow point bullet expanded on impact and blew him apart.

She quickly took out her husband's best friend with a second shot before anyone even thought to move for cover.

She killed the third detective as he turned to run.

She picked up the three shell casings, made sure she had left nothing else where she had fired, brushed around the dirt to kill any shoe prints, then put the gun back in the case open on the back seat of the car and headed down the road.

She turned away from the police and then worked her way slowly back toward the mall.

She parked the Ford sedan next to her Jeep again. Then she transferred the disguise bag and everything into her car and put the rifle back under the back seats.

She climbed into her Jeep and turned on a high-tech scanner she had in her purse that told her if any camera was watching at all.

Nothing, as she had known for this area of the large mall parking lot.

She quickly pulled off her disguise and tossed them into the bag, zipping it up and putting it on the floor behind her driver's seat.

Then she took off the thin, transparent gloves she had been wearing that were embedded with fake fingerprints and stuck those in the pocket of her jeans.

She hit almost no traffic on the short drive home.

That was nice. Her job was done now.

All she had to do was make sure nothing came back toward her and get paid before moving on and vanishing into the next job.

CHAPTER TEN

JEAN WATCHED AS Mary Jo pulled into her garage and the door slid shut. She had been gone for just over forty minutes.

What was she up to? Where was Sam?

Jean really, really wanted to just go bang on the door and ask what had happened to Sam, but that would blow her cover completely.

But honestly, she wasn't sure that her cover wasn't already blown. She needed to be prepared for that possibility.

She quickly went out to her garage and clicked open yet another secret panel behind some boxes she stored there. Sam had been handy with tools, but he had no idea how good she was as well, and she never let on that she was a master carpenter who could build just about anything she needed.

In the panel was what she called her "go bag" meaning guns, clothes, an extra pair of shoes, fake passports and drivers' licenses, and some rolls of cash.

She also had two different full face and hair disguises in the bag.

If she needed to go, there was a way she could go under the hot tub, through an opening in the deck siding and through their fence and into the neighbor's back yard.

She kept an SUV gassed and stored in a self-storage place five blocks away.

She closed up the panel and put her go bag near her back door where she could get it on a run, then went back into the living room and sat, watching Mary Jo's house.

She had often sat in the same chair, watching for her target, Chief Hanson, to get home. She knew their routines as well as her own. He should be home by now, but clearly he hadn't come in yet.

A few moments later the garage door on Mary Jo's garage opened again and she backed out. The windows on Mary Jo's Jeep were tinted, so no way Jean could tell what she had.

And still no way that Jean could try to go into that house to investigate what happened to Sam.

She watched Mary Jo drive away, then stood and went into her kitchen to make a quick sandwich and grab a bottle of a sports drink.

This was going to be a long night.

A very long night.

CHAPTER ELEVEN

BACK AT HOME after her run to the rock quarry, Mary Jo put back on the fake fingerprint gloves and pulled out two more black garbage bags full of weekly trash from the kitchen, including a bunch of stuff she had tossed out of the fridge after wiping prints and putting the fake prints on the stuff.

She got the rifle from the car and broke it down and put parts in three bags, wearing her fake fingerprint gloves as she did.

Then she took parts of her costume and spread them through the garbage as well. And she made sure that there was nothing in the bags that would lead to her in this home in any fashion.

Next, she headed back to the landfill, made some mention to the man taking her money that it was her second trip because she was cleaning house. He didn't care. He was about to close up for the night.

She tossed the three bags over the edge and into the stinking mess of the landfill.

A moment later the large grader covered all three with a layer of dirt.

She could feel the slight relief and excitement course through her.

A job finished.

Her tracks completely covered.

Nothing could lead anyone back to her for the deaths today.

So Mary Jo headed home once again.

She had played the happy wife for the last year, now she had a new part to play for a while.

She had to play the part of the grieving widow.

Sam's wife would be grieving as well tonight.

CHAPTER TWELVE

AFTER MARY JO came back once again, Jean went to the panel in her closet and pulled out a police scanner. If Sam miraculously showed up, she would explain where it had come from, if she couldn't hide it in time.

Or she would just kill him and abort this job. Something clearly had happened and she had no idea what.

She was shocked when she turned on the police scanner. It was going crazy.

It took her a few minutes to piece it all together, but it seemed that while responding to the report of a body in the rock quarry (more than likely Sam's) just outside of town, Chief Hanson had been killed along with two other detectives by sniper fire.

No suspects at all.

"Well I'll be a bitch's bastard," Jean said, standing and pacing in the living room.

She knew exactly what had happened. The bastard who had hired her to kill Chief Hanson had hired another assassin as well.

And the other assassin had used poor Sam as bait to get Chief Hansen into a dead zone at the bottom of a rock quarry for an easy kill.

And that other assassin was none other than Mary Jo, the chief's wife.

Jean had married or slept with her target many times over the centuries. It was a very easy way to get close enough to the target to know how to deal with finding an easy way to kill the target and not have any evidence lead to you.

And sometimes it was actually fun.

Jean stared down the quiet suburban street at Mary Jo's house. Jean was sure that Mary Jo had no idea that she had just killed the husband of another assassin. Jean wouldn't hold that against Mary Jo, but it was something just not done.

In fact, assassins never worked together. Or as far as Jean knew they didn't.

And they were never hired for the same job and never sent to compete. Jean had no doubt that the bastard who had hired the both of them was going to pay and pay large.

But now Jean had to figure out if she was going to let Mary Jo know she was part of the same ancient order of assassins. Over the centuries, Jean had met fewer than twenty of the other assassins. All of them had been women like her, most were small, like her and Mary Jo.

And all looked like they could never hurt a flea.

Jean had no idea if there were male assassins with the order. She had never asked. In fact, the last time she communicated with anyone directly in the organization had been long before the First World War. The assassins were just independent contractors, living and working on their own terms and in their own ways. Killing when the money was good enough, but never just for sport.

The bastard that had hired them both was going to pay. But the question now was should Jean contact Mary Jo or just let events play out?

At the moment, she needed to just let events play out. She had no other choice. She had to play the surprised and suddenly grieving widow.

And she had to play it perfectly.

She wasn't worried. It was a part she had played many, many times over the centuries.

PART THREE
Complication

CHAPTER THIRTEEN

JEAN HAD BEEN suspicious of the hug from the young woman cop from the instant it happened. It had gone on far too long.

Not that Jean minded being hugged by a woman. In fact, she liked a lot more from women than just hugs. But the cop's hug had been inappropriate and bumbling. Like a high school boy on his first date.

Even with the two cops giving her the news that her husband had been killed, that hug had been wrong.

Jean had played out the scene perfectly, pretending to melt into a pile and then slowly recovering when told her about her husband.

As the cops left, that was when the woman cop had hugged her.

So Jean watched the two cops go down the street to give the same news to Mary Jo. When they entered Mary Jo's home, Jean quickly went to her closet and got out a scanner.

The bitch had planted an audio scanner in her collar. The scanner was powerful and tiny.

Very tiny. But not top of the line by any means.

Amateur.

The rest of the house was clear.

Jean quickly went to the garage and flicked a hidden switch there. A small screen appeared and she knew instantly that there were no scans or cameras around her house or in the general neighborhood.

Jean left the bug in place in her collar and went back to the living room to watch until the two cops left Mary Jo's house. Someone was clearly trying to double-cross her and more than likely Mary Jo.

To play into the script that whoever was listening would expect, she broke into sobs and tears a few times. She really didn't feel bad for losing poor old Sam. He had been a nice guy. Not much more.

So what was an amateur doing planting a bug on her? And how did the young cop even know about her?

More than likely the young cop thought of herself as a killer and had been told, more than likely by the client, that Jean and Mary Jo needed to be eliminated.

How the client had gotten that information was the problem that also needed to be solved.

The young cop was an amateur, clearly not from the order.

Jean quickly scribbled some notes on a yellow legal pad after the two cops drove away, then headed out the front door.

It seemed the question of when or if she should tell Mary Jo she had also been hired for this target had been answered.

Now was the time.

She couldn't believe Mary Jo wouldn't have spotted the bug, but better safe than sorry.

And one of them would need to deal with the problem.

CHAPTER FOURTEEN

MARY JO WAS watching television when the expected two uniformed cops came to her door.

One was a woman cop who seemed to be almost in tears.

They told Mary Jo the news and she broke down as the two cops expected her to do.

They asked Mary Jo if there was anything they could do and Mary Jo told them she had a sister who would come over and stay with her. She didn't, but the two cops bought it.

Then the woman cop hugged her harder and longer than was necessary and gave Mary Jo her card for anything she needed.

Mary Jo wondered if her good old husband had been getting a little of that on the side. He didn't seem to be the type. But that had sure been a strange hug.

Mary Jo was about to go fix herself that long-overdue second Screwdriver after the two officers left when her alarm bells went off.

Instead, she went to her bedroom, all the while pretending to be distraught.

She quickly used a scanner she kept hidden in the back of her dresser drawer to check for audio and visual bugs in the house or surrounding neighborhood.

The woman officer had planted one all right, under the back collar of her blouse.

Audio only.

Not high grade.

There were no other bugs in the house or around the house or neighborhood.

No young rookie cop would do that, especially so quickly after the entire

department was tossed into panic mode. Besides, there was no reason to suspect Mary Jo.

That girl worked for someone outside the department. More than likely the same idiot who had paid Mary Jo to kill her husband and would pay a second half as soon as she reported in to him.

And the stupid woman was a rookie at the job. Not a member of the order, that was for sure.

Mary Jo shook her head.

How the bastard had known it was her was a question she would deal with later.

For now the bastard who had hired her would pay a far higher sum. You didn't try to double-cross Mary Jo. Not ever. The idiot who had hired her had no idea the order of assassins even existed.

So he thought Mary Jo would be easy to get rid of.

Keeping up the act of a distraught wife for the bug, she put on thin, clear gloves and took from what looked like a perfume bottle a small drop of fluid on a pad. She carefully wrapped the pad in a tiny bag and stuck it in her pocket. It was an odorless, untraceable poison that would kill anyone who touched it within five minutes.

She took off the glove and put it in her pocket as well.

She was about to call the young officer when there was a knock at her door.

She glanced at the security feed to see the face of Sam's recently widowed wife.

She was a beautiful woman. Wow, just stunning.

But what the hell was she doing here at this point in time?

Mary Jo, making sure her tears were in place on her face, opened up the door.

The woman facing her was about Mary Jo's size and so beautiful it took Mary Jo's

breath away. The woman had deep green eyes that seemed to see everything and a body that under other circumstances, Mary Jo wouldn't have minded spending time exploring.

A lot of time, actually.

It took Mary Jo a moment to say to the woman, who was also crying, "I'm sorry, this is a bad time."

The woman nodded. "I know. I just want to say how sorry I am for your loss."

At that moment, the woman standing in the door put up a finger to her lips for Mary Jo to say nothing more, then held up a yellow legal pad against her chest for only Mary Jo to see.

On the pad it said:

I am being monitored. Audio only as far as I can tell. I assume you are as well. The young woman cop who gave us the news about our husbands planted the bug. I am also with the order.

Mary Jo felt stunned.

Completely stunned.

Clearly the jerk that had hired her had hired another assassin for the same target.

Mary Jo nodded as the other woman pointed to her collar, the same place the cop had planted the bug on Mary Jo.

"Thank you," Mary Jo said, following along on the speaking script they clearly were both on now. "Can you come in for a moment?"

The woman nodded. "Only a moment."

"I am sorry for your loss as well," Mary Jo said as she closed the door. "It is horrid what has happened."

The moment the door closed the other woman stopped actually crying and so did Mary Jo.

The woman said, "Thank you." Her voice sounding like she was barely holding it together while her face clearly wasn't following the part.

The woman turned the page on the notebook. There Mary Jo read:

My guess is we were both hired for the same target. Now clearly someone is trying to double-cross us both. Clear us both out of the picture.

Mary Jo nodded and said aloud, "Do you have family to come and help you?"

"I have a sister," the other woman said. "By the way, my name is Jean."

"I am Mary Jo," Mary Jo said, taking the pad from Jean's hand and the pen. Mary Jo quickly wrote:

Discovered the bug. About to call the bitch who planted it and deal with her.

"I'm so sorry we had to meet like this," Jean said, smiling at Mary Jo.

Mary Jo had a hunch she would come to love that smile.

"I am too," Mary Jo said as Jean wrote on the pad:

Need help?

Mary Jo shook her head.

"Maybe through these trying times we can be of support to one another," Jean said.

"Thank you," Mary Jo said, taking back the pad. "I would like that."

She wrote on the pad:

Got this. The little bitch cop will be dead in thirty minutes.

Jean nodded. "Good."

It was clear to Mary Jo she meant both the seeing each other and taking care of the bug planter.

Jean took the pad back and wrote:

I will contact the order and tell them what happened. Ask how someone could track us...

"Thank you," Mary Jo said, nodding.

Jean opened the door, leaving the pad of paper. Then with a smile at Mary Jo, Jean said, "We both have things we need to take care of."

She indicated her collar and then turned to go down the sidewalk and back to her home.

Mary Jo just stood there for a moment, watching her go before closing the door.

So someone had hired two assassins to kill the same target. And then tried to double-cross both.

What an idiot.

The guy was going to pay and pay large. And pay them both.

But first Mary Jo had to take care of the immediate problem of the bug and the young cop who planted it.

CHAPTER FIFTEEN

JEAN WAS STUNNED at the reaction she had had seeing Mary Jo up close. The woman was stunningly beautiful. And her dark brown eyes were something Jean knew she could stare into for a very long time.

Mary Jo seemed to be shorter than Jean, if that was possible, and, of course, in perfect shape. And Mary Jo had what looked to be perfect, smooth skin.

The reaction to Mary Jo had been unexpected and had actually caught Jean by surprise, something that was difficult to do in general.

She walked slowly along the sidewalk toward her own home. All she could think about was seeing Mary Jo without clothes on, sliding into Jean's hot tub on her back deck.

The idea of that just made Jean short of breath.

She pretended to sob slightly for the bug on her collar, but the sob was more of a shudder of anticipation.

She had met very, very few other assassins over the years. And her last real relationship (not counting the fake marriages to the likes of poor old Sam) had been almost a hundred years earlier. She had fallen completely in love with a woman named Sarah and the two of them had traveled the world as traveling companions. Sarah had died of consumption after fifteen years together.

A wonderful fifteen years.

And never since that point had Jean felt an attraction toward another person like she had felt this evening for Mary Jo.

This could be a problem, of that there was no doubt. There were no rules in the order forbidding a relationship between two assassins, and Jean actually had no idea if Mary Jo would even be attracted to her.

But for the moment, they were both stuck three houses apart in the same neighborhood in the same small New York town, playing the same grieving widow part.

So it would be interesting.

Jean reached her front door and tried to shake the image of a naked Mary Jo from her mind.

That was a hard image to clear.

CHAPTER SIXTEEN

MARY JO CLOSED the door on Jean and stood and thought for a moment. This had gone from a simple target to really twisted in very quick order. Clearly the client who had hired her hadn't trusted she would get the job done, so he had hired another assassin.

Or maybe Mary Jo had been the backup and just got to the target first. No way of knowing.

And then the client had hired a rookie killer to take care of both of them after the job was finished.

This needed to get cleaned up and cleaned up fast.

Mary Jo took a deep breath, dropped back into acting for the bug in her collar and called the young woman officer's number on the card.

"I want to see my husband."

"I don't think that is such a good idea," the young woman cop said.

Mary Jo nodded. Both of them were right on the script that Mary Jo knew would happen.

"I'm coming to the station anyway," Mary Jo said, and hung up.

Mary Jo smiled. That would screw with the young twit's mind.

Ten minutes later, Mary Jo pulled up out front after pretending to cry most of the way to the station so that anyone listening to the bug wouldn't be shocked.

When she parked, Mary Jo spent a moment putting on the one clear glove and getting the poison solution ready to go, all the while pretending to cry.

The young woman cop met Mary Jo at the big double door. Concrete steps led up into the front desk of the station. Around them the night was still warm, without even a breeze.

"I don't think this is a good idea," the young cop said. "Your husband was shot and they need to do an autopsy."

Mary Jo had the poison pad in her hand and her hands were covered in the thin, almost invisible gloves with fake fingerprints.

"You may be right," Mary Jo said after a moment, keeping on the script that she expected. "I don't know what I am thinking."

She gave the young cop a hug, rubbing the pad along her neck before backing away.

"I'm sure sorry," Mary Jo said.

"It's understandable," the young cop said.

The young woman cop had no idea what Mary Jo really meant and that actually, she wasn't sorry at all.

Suddenly the young cop looked pale and swallowed hard.

Mary Jo took her under her arm and turned to take her up the three steps and into the station. The drug was very fast acting and this woman would be dead in five minutes tops.

As she helped the woman up the steps, Mary Jo pretended to pause and stagger a moment. As she did, hidden from view from any camera, she slipped off the gloves and tossed them into a garbage can near the front door. The can was full of Burger King cups and food bags from the nearby fast food restaurant.

The poison wouldn't last in the air like that for another thirty minutes and the gloves would dissolve in two hours.

"Help!" Mary Jo shouted to the officers inside as she opened the door. "She just collapsed into my arms on the front steps."

Two cops ran to grab the young officer, then a third nodded to Mary Jo and offered his sincere condolences. Clearly the guy recognized her as the wife of the now-dead chief.

Mary Jo broke into sobs, as scheduled for her part of this passion play.

They let her sit in a back office and calm down before having an officer drive her home.

Then, as she closed her front door, Mary Jo killed the bug on her blouse and made sure the rest of her house and the nearby houses were clean of all recording and electronic devices and cameras.

Everything was clean.

She dug out a burner phone from a fake bottom of her purse and dialed a number.

"Yeah," a voice on the other end said.

"Target is dead. The remainder of my fee has tripled because of your attempt at a double-cross. If the money is not in the agreed-upon account by this time tomorrow afternoon, you know the consequences."

"You can't threaten me," the voice said.

"I know where you live, where your children sleep, where your wife loves to eat sushi," Mary Jo said, keeping her voice calm and low and slightly angry. "I am patient, invisible, and you hired me because I get the job done. The job you hired me to do is done. The price is now four times my fee. Please do not fail me."

Then she hung up, put the phone in a baggy and smashed it into tiny pieces.

Then she put some bleach and a few drops of a special solution into the baggy, sealed it, and tossed it into the trashcan outside. The entire thing would be a puddle of goo in the bottom of the can in an hour.

She then took a deep breath.

Finally, it was time.

She took out the pitcher of orange juice, a highball glass, and the vodka. She filled the glass with ice, added a good solid shot of vodka, then filled the rest of the glass with orange juice.

Then she put everything away before sipping the wonderful drink.

Perfect.

Just perfect.

Maybe, just maybe, a little later, she might just have one more.

And after the funerals, maybe she and Jean might share a few drinks as well.

After all, grieving widows could be forgiven a drink or two.

PART FOUR
Gaining a Partner

CHAPTER SEVENTEEN

WHEN JEAN SAW Mary Jo be dropped off at her home by an officer, she knew the young cop was dead. On the police scanners, the call for an ambulance for the police station had gone out

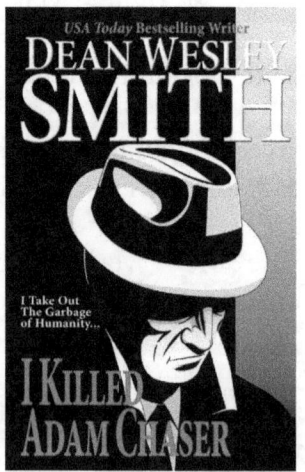

at the point Mary Jo would have reached the police station.

Jean smiled and took the bug from her collar and smashed it, then put it into a solution that would dissolve it within an hour.

She then took out a burner phone that she had kept hidden in the kitchen, taped up underneath a lower cabinet shelf. She dialed the only number on the phone and when a man answered, she said simply.

"Target is dead. I am not sure why you tried to double-cross me, but my fee for such action on your part has now doubled. I will expect it in the account shortly."

"You can't threaten me," the man said, his voice full of bluster with no real power behind it.

"You obviously don't know who exactly you hired," Jean said, keeping her voice low and level. "My fee is now four times. I do not expect to be disappointed."

Jean clicked off the phone, put it in a very heavy plastic bag and then smashed it until it was dust. Then she poured the solution with the bug in it into the plastic bag, wrapped it all in an old rag, and dropped it in the bottom of her garbage can in her garage.

In an hour the entire thing would be nothing more than a gooey mess inside the cloth.

She laughed as she went back into the house. She had a hunch that Mary Jo had just called the same guy and said basically the same thing. The only issue was if they had been hired for the same target by two different clients.

And, of course, she and Mary Jo both had an issue since the young cop had clearly known about both of them. So others might as well and know where they both lived.

Precautions were in order.

Jean went into her bedroom and into her secret stash behind her closet. There she took out a very special phone. She had never used the phone which had been handed to her four years ago for direct contact with the ancient order of assassins. The organization had no real name, never had.

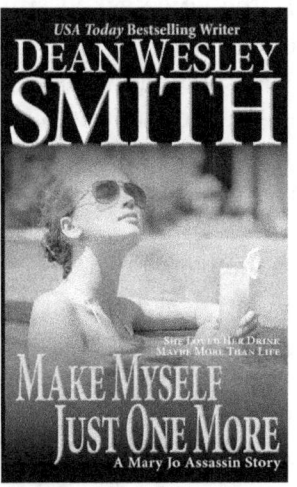

Some Classic Dean Wesley Smith Stories
Available at your favorite booksellers.

And in thousands of years, Jean had seldom had need to actually speak to anyone in the order.

She checked to make sure there was no tracking on the phone, then hit the number four.

A moment later a recorded voice said, "State your name."

Jean said simply, "Freyja Mist."

A moment later a human voice said simply, "May I be of service?"

"Were two assassins hired for the same target in upstate New York just over a year ago?"

"We keep no records. But such occurrences have happened throughout time. It would be possible."

"Understood," Jean said. "Both assassins were then targeted by an amateur killer after the target was eliminated. How could such a thing happen? No contact with the client was made by either assassin."

Jean knew she was speaking for Mary Jo, but she had no doubt Mary Jo would have had no reason outside the normal channels to contact the client in any way.

Silence greeted Jean's question.

Finally the voice asked simply, "Has the threat been eliminated?"

"The immediate threat has, yes."

"The phone you hold will ring exactly twenty-four hours from this moment. I will have information for you at that point."

The phone went dead.

Jean glanced at her watch, then put the phone away and closed the secret panel on her closet.

That was done.

She set all proximity alarms around the house, made sure she had weapons in various places throughout the house, then took a deep breath.

"I need a drink."

CHAPTER EIGHTEEN

MARY JO HATED everything to do with the funeral for her husband. The entire town was a mess, actually. Three detectives killed, another young cop drops dead, a writer murdered for no reason.

Mary Jo hated the sitting and pretending to mourn, she hated the questions that the poor cops had to ask and kept apologizing for asking.

And she really hated not being free to move around the way she wanted. This was always the worst part about killing a target you had made into a spouse.

Finally, a week after the funerals, things seemed to be starting to calm down. But she didn't drop her guard at all, since somehow some amateur killer had found out about her and Jean.

She had no idea how that might have happened, but she would figure it out. Something she or Jean had done had let the client on to who they were and where they were.

On the ninth day after the funeral, she decided she needed to get some answers. So just after ten in the morning, with a bottle of the Absolute Crystal vodka and a thermos of orange juice in a bag, she headed three houses up the block to Jean's house.

Jean answered the door after one knock, smiling and offering for her to come in.

Mary Jo for an instant had trouble even moving. She had thought a lot about Jean over the last two weeks, but now, facing her, she was more beautiful than Mary Jo remembered.

This morning Jean's blonde hair was pulled back and her green eyes seemed to shine. She had on no make-up and wore a white blouse with a sports bra under it and jeans. She was also barefoot, something that Mary Jo did around her house as well.

"I come bearing drinks," Mary Jo said, patting her bag.

"Ah, a neighbor after my own heart," Jean said, leading the way through the entry and toward the modern kitchen beyond.

Actually Mary Jo wanted to say she was after Jean's body, but instead said nothing and settled for watching the wonderful ass of the woman in front of her. She normally never looked at women's asses, instead preferring eyes and smiles and hands. But for Jean, Mary Jo was making an exception.

Mary Jo pulled out the bottle of vodka and the thermos of orange juice and set them on the counter.

Mary Jo had left the vodka in its original container now that she didn't need to hide it from her husband.

"I see you have great taste in vodka," Jean said, smiling.

"You like screwdrivers?"

Jean's eyes lit up and then Jean laughed, a wonderful sound Mary Jo could come to enjoy. "My favorite drink. How did you know?"

"My favorite as well," Mary Jo said, laughing along with Jean.

And what little bit of tension between the two eased as Jean got them tall tumblers and filled them with ice and Mary Jo poured their drinks.

They took the drinks and went to the kitchen table and sat down, both sipping at the same time.

"So," Mary Jo said. "You have this house protected?"

Jean nodded, taking a second sip. "Completely. No one can hear a word we say or get close enough to cause any damage."

"So who hired you?" Mary Jo asked. Then she went ahead and volunteered her client's name. "Stanton Cobble the Third was mine."

Jean nodded. "Same jerk. And I bumped his final fee to four times the two million he owed me and he paid me only a million."

Mary Jo laughed. "I did the same and the guy only paid me a million as well."

Jean smiled as she took another sip from her drink. "Seems we have some fees to extract from a client."

"And teach him a lesson as well," Mary Jo said. "But first we have to figure out how he found us."

"The phones we used to call him," Jean said so easily that Mary Jo was surprised.

Jean smiled. "I called the order and asked them if two of us had been hired for the same client."

"They don't keep records so they wouldn't know," Mary Jo said, surprised that Jean had called the order. That wasn't something she had done in the modern world.

"I told them about our rookie assassin and they called me back with how the client would have found us. Seems he had someone trace the phones somehow to our homes."

"So more than one person knows about our involvement in the events of a few weeks ago?" Mary Jo asked. She wasn't happy at all with the sounds of that.

"The order says no," Jean said. "They traced it all, so we are clear there, but I am taking no chances just in case."

"I agree," Mary Jo said. "Very slow. Guard completely up."

"So next spring we think of moving on the client?" Jean asked.

"Next spring," Mary Jo said, nodding and smiling. "Give the bastard time to relax a little. And us time to make sure the order is right about only the one amateur."

"And to plan," Jean said. "Sometimes that's half the fun."

"I agree," Mary Jo said, raising her glass. "And sure sorry about killing your husband?"

Jean laughed. "Nice guy, dull in bed, and a mediocre writer. I was going to have to kill him when I moved on the target anyway, so I owe you one."

"Ouch," Mary Jo said, laughing. "Nice, dull, and mediocre. I hope you didn't put that on his tombstone."

Jean laughed again and Mary Jo just watched and listened and enjoyed. She hadn't been looking forward to the winter, but having Jean so close was sure going to make it a lot more fun.

PART FIVE
A Winter Hot Tub

CHAPTER NINETEEN

JEAN NEVER UNDERSTOOD why someone with money seemed to automatically think they could get away with anything, including murder. Granted, enough money bought a murder.

And even more money bought her skills for the murder.

But it never bought a double-cross.

Over the thousands of years that she had been an assassin in the order, she had had clients who had not paid her after she finished a job. That client always paid dearly with his or her life and the lives of those that were treasured by the person doing the double-crossing.

To Jean, a deal was a deal. Yet often people with money thought otherwise.

So the idiot who had not only double-crossed her, but another assassin from the order at the same time, would pay dearly.

In time.

She and Mary Jo were very, very patient killers.

And they both liked to plan.

In fact, they loved to plan.

So they settled into their homes for the winter, still both living the grieving-widow routines when out in public. By the time two months had passed since what she and Mary Jo laughingly called "The Event," they were spending more and more time together. They hadn't gone out into public at all together, and Jean had gone back to work after two weeks to keep up appearances.

But six nights a week they had dinner together. Every other night Jean cooked, every other night Mary Jo cooked.

Mary Jo could stir up pasta dishes that could make a person's mouth water from a hundred paces. And Jean loved to cook with fish and chicken. Both of them, over the centuries, had learned the art of cooking and now they both had someone to appreciate their skills.

And they could talk about where they learned what and not hide the fact of their ages and their experiences. To Jean, that was such a wonderful treat.

Before, her life had been closed off, something to never be talked about. Now, she and Mary Jo both had thousands of years of experiences and learning to talk about with each other.

And wonderful food to share.

In fact, most of the purchases Jean had made in the last month were for better kitchen cookware.

And Mary Jo had been doing the same.

But what Jean had loved the most about the last two months was the flirting and staring into Mary Jo's dark brown eyes. At times, when Mary Jo left, Jean had just wanted to stop her and kiss her. But as in murder, Jean was very patient in love as well.

Frustrated, but patient.

Just over two months after "The Event," Mary Jo had gone into New York City to do their first scouting of Stanton Cobble and his life. When she returned on the late train just after eight, Jean met her at the station and drove her home.

"Dinner at my place if you're hungry?" Jean said as they left the station. She had hoped Mary Jo would be hungry, so had done some prep work on a special chicken dish Jean had learned a few hundred years back in Italy.

"Famished," Mary Jo said, easing her shoulders around.

Jean could hear the cracking in Mary Jo's back.

Jean smiled. Long train rides stiffened up her muscles like that as well.

"You sound like you could use a dip in the hot tub after that ride," Jean said, trying to focus on driving and not think about seeing Mary Jo without clothes on.

"That sounds heavenly," Mary Jo said, smiling. "But dinner first. I got a lot to tell you about our idiot target."

"Dinner will be ready in forty-five minutes after we get home," Jean said.

Mary Jo sighed and nodded. "Thanks. That sounds wonderful. Gives me time to take a quick shower and change clothes."

Again, it took every ounce of training for Jean to keep her eyes on the road and her attention on her driving instead of imagining Mary Jo without clothes on.

Somehow she managed to get them both home safely.

Somehow.

CHAPTER TWENTY

AFTER A SHOWER and fresh clothes—jeans, a sports bra and a tan silk blouse—Mary Jo felt almost human again. The four-hour train ride from the city could take the energy out of anyone. She was in shape and exercised every day, but that trip still was draining, especially since she had caught the early morning train at five.

She had only needed six hours in the city to get a sense of how good-old-idiot Stanton was living. In just two months, he was clearly starting to relax his guard.

And it seemed his wife never had been guarded. And his parents were open targets. Both Mary Jo and Jean had studied Stanton's activities before moving north to do their hired job. Now the idiot hadn't seemed to alter much of anything.

He still met his mistress two afternoons a week, still had dinner at the same restaurants, still lived in the same penthouse apartment overlooking Central Park.

But the key was going to be to get his money and disgrace him without actually killing him. Killing him, both Mary Jo and Jean had decided, would be too easy on him.

He needed to suffer and suffer he would.

They just didn't know how yet.

Jean had been a dream friend, getting up early and taking Mary Jo to the train station and then picking her up and offering dinner.

And the idea of crawling into Jean's hot tub after dinner had Mary Jo so distracted, she could hardly think. For two months now, Mary Jo had been flirting with Jean and loving every minute of it.

And just about every night Mary Jo went to sleep in her own bed wishing Jean was beside her. It had been a very long time since Mary Jo had felt anything like this for another person. And she was enjoying it immensely.

Maybe tonight, finally, they could take this budding relationship and friendship to the next level.

She sure hoped so.

When Mary Jo did her standard knock and then let herself into Jean's comfortable living room, the fantastic smell hit her. Rich, thick garlic and oregano spice smell seemed to just thicken the air like a sweet sauce over thin pasta.

"Wow, does that smell wonderful!" Mary Jo said, heading for the kitchen.

"Thanks," Jean said, turning from the stove and smiling at Mary Jo as she entered. "Fresh orange juice in the fridge."

Jean looked as heavenly as always tonight, with tight jeans, a green blouse with the sleeves rolled up, and a full dark apron tied in the back. Mary Jo just stared at her for a moment before heading to the fridge to pour them both a vodka and orange juice to go with their dinner.

She found it sort of funny that even though both of them were gourmet-level cooks, neither of them cared much for wine with their dinners. It was only one of many things they had in common they had discovered over the last few months.

Mary Jo found it really amazing that Jean's favorite drink by far was a screwdriver, made the same way Mary Jo liked them. How could she not love another assassin that drank screwdrivers?

Dinner was heavenly. The chicken in the marinara sauce seemed to melt in her mouth with a burst of spice and sweetness she couldn't believe. Sautéed fresh vegetables in light olive oil were a perfect addition.

As they ate and then sipped their drinks, Mary Jo filled Jean in on how idiot Stanton hadn't changed much of his ways at all to protect himself. Jean just shook her head at the stupidity.

"He hires two of us to kill his target," Jean said, disgusted, "then shorts us and doesn't think we'll come after him. One of the stupidest clients I have ever worked for."

Mary Jo laughed and raised her glass to that one. "I suppose he figures that paying us half our final original payment would be enough."

"He thought wrong," Jean said. She laughed as well.

Then Jean looked into Mary Jo's eyes. "You look exhausted. How about that hot tub to get you relaxed so you can get some sleep."

Mary Jo could feel her heart race and she had no doubt her face flushed a little, but Jean's face was flushed as well.

"I thought you would never ask," Mary Jo said. "But dishes first."

"Not a chance," Jean said, standing and offering her hand to Mary Jo.

Mary Jo smiled and stood and took Jean's hand.

It was like a small electrical shock had hit her. Jean's hand felt firm and powerful and at the same time soft and wonderful. And her hand fit perfectly in Mary Jo's hand.

Jean flushed slightly and then pulling Mary Jo toward the back patio door, led the way to the hot tub.

Two large bath towels were on a bench there and the lights were off on the back porch, but there was enough light to see where they were going from the kitchen lights.

The evening air had a crisp fall bite to it and a smell of dry pine and leaves.

"Get undressed and I'll get the tub ready," Jean said, letting go of Mary Jo's hand and lifting the cover back off the hot tub.

As Mary Jo unbuttoned her blouse, Jean slid the cover back and off the tub into a holder against the house.

Mary Jo had her blouse unbuttoned and mostly off when Jean turned around and just stopped and stared.

Mary Jo liked how Jean was looking at her.

Liked it a lot.

She unzipped her jeans and slipped them off quickly, standing there in the half-light of the fall evening in just her sports bra and thin underwear.

"You look fantastic," Jean said, her breath not much more than a whisper.

"Thank you," Mary Jo said. "Now your turn. I've been dreaming about seeing you naked since we met."

Jean smiled and unbuttoned her blouse as Mary Jo watched Jean's wonderful hands at work.

Then Jean slid off her jeans and just stood there, smiling.

Jean had on a lace bra and matching lace panties. She was flat stunning.

"Damn, that's better than I had dreamed," Mary Jo said. It was everything she could do to catch her breath.

Finally Mary Jo forced herself to move and took off her bra. Then slipped off her panties.

Jean just stared.

Then Jean took off her underwear and Mary Jo just stared.

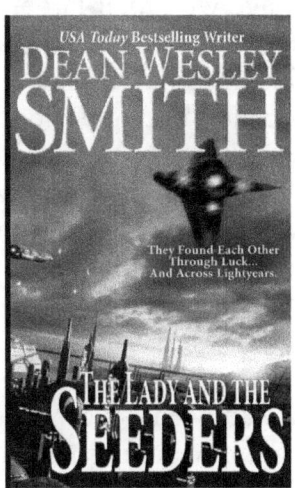

And then finally Mary Jo got herself to move.

Not into the hot tub, but into Jean's welcoming arms.

Right were Mary Jo knew she belonged.

CHAPTER TWENTY-ONE

AFTER THAT FIRST night, Mary Jo stayed at Jean's house one night and Jean stayed at Mary Jo's house the next. That lasted for exactly one week before Mary Jo had just laughed and said they were being silly for no reason.

She wanted to live with Jean, be close to her every night, wake up with her every morning, and she didn't care where that was, honestly.

Jean had said she wanted to live with Mary Jo. And the hot tub was at Jean's house, as well as Jean's house being easier to guard.

And Mary Jo had nothing from her marriage with their target that she much cared about. She was used to leaving behind material things. Her house, as they called it, really didn't feel like her house.

So three months after the event, Mary Jo, with Jean helping, cleared out most of her closets and took over a second bedroom in Jean's house.

It felt wonderful.

And it felt right.

It had been far, far longer than Mary Jo wanted to admit since the last time she had been in love with anyone. And one night in the hot tub, Jean had confided that for her it had been almost a century since she had felt real love.

But there was no doubt to either of them that they both were now in love.

And enjoying it.

Mary Jo couldn't believe how lucky she had gotten.

They had decided that Mary Jo should just keep her house and the pretense of living there for the small town. But Mary Jo had a hunch the town would soon know what was happening. And she and Jean didn't care that much anymore. They had played their parts just fine after their husbands' deaths.

Time to move forward.

So one cold but clear December evening, with the snow crunching under their boots, they went for dinner together at a wonderful Italian restaurant just off of Main Street.

Everyone they met greeted them cheerfully.

And not only was the dinner wonderful, but the conversation lively and the sex afterward mind-blowing.

So they made going out together a habit twice a week. Mary Jo didn't even see a suspicious eyebrow raised.

On the last working day of January, Jean quit her job. They no longer needed to keep up pretenses about not being together and the following month, Mary Jo sold her house.

They were officially a couple.

And every day that thought surprised Mary Jo.

The fall and winter had been almost magical for Mary Jo. She had never imagined falling so perfectly in love with anyone else, let alone another assassin. She loved everything about Jean, including her perfect body and her sharp mind.

But most of all, she loved Jean's passion for her work and keeping herself in shape.

Both of them exercised and trained three hours a day, often together, sometimes alone. Mary Jo had no doubt at all that Jean was one of the deadliest assassins ever to be in the order.

And on top of that, Jean never seemed to tire of vodka and orange juice. What was there not to love?

Mary Jo never tired of watching Jean get undressed to climb into the hot tub.

And Jean seemed to never tire of exploring Mary Jo's body.

They really were a perfect match.

Something Mary Jo would have sworn impossible just a year earlier.

CHAPTER TWENTY-TWO

JEAN HAD NEVER wanted the last six months to end, and she hoped they wouldn't. But there was no doubt she and Mary Jo needed to get going with their plan to move on their target.

All winter long they had worked on the plan, sometimes over dinner, sometimes sitting in the hot tub while sipping vodka and orange juice.

And the plan was a good one.

So during a wonderful dinner of Italian-spiced chicken laid over a bed of green, smothered in a cheese combination, Jean finally turned to the woman she had fallen madly in love with.

"I think it's time."

Mary Jo nodded and didn't look up from her salad. "I agree."

The first part of the plan was that Mary Jo would head into the city and live in an apartment they had rented across from a condo their target owned and used for affairs.

Jean would stay behind and sell the house and dispose of everything before moving into the city to another apartment they had rented close to the target's large apartment near Central Park.

They both figured it would take at least three months, maybe longer, before they could move on the target. The tricky part was going to be the banking.

But Jean was convinced their plan on that would work.

The only thing Jean didn't like about the plan was being separated from Mary Jo. And Mary Jo had said that was what she didn't like as well.

But Jean knew, just as Mary Jo did, that if they were going to have a long-term relationship, they were both going to need to go their own ways at times to do their jobs.

That knowledge didn't make it any easier.

But what did make it easier was the fact that they had worked on this plan together. It had been fun, actually, and Jean had to admit their plan was a lot better than anything she could have come up with alone. Mary Jo just had a stunning mind for knowing how to get inside a person's life to get close to a target.

So if this worked out, maybe, just maybe, going down the road, they would stay together more than they would be apart. Work together more. At least that's what Jean wanted.

Mary Jo seemed to be focusing on her dinner, clearly not wanting to look up at Jean.

Jean leaned forward and touched Mary Jo's hand. Mary Jo finally looked up, her deep brown eyes worried and sad.

"You know I love you, don't you?" Jean said.

Mary Jo nodded. "I love you as well."

"And if I have anything to say about it," Jean said, smiling, "we're going to be sharing a hot tub and drinks for a long time into the future."

"Now that's a plan I like," Mary Jo said.

Jean watched as Mary Jo took a deep breath and then smiled. "I'll head out in the morning, call you when I get settled there as we discussed."

"I'll get started on disposing of all this stuff and getting the house listed," Jean said. "And then join you in the city."

"Taking this jerk down is going to be fun," Mary Jo said, smiling.

Jean laughed and stood and went around the small dining table to kiss Mary Jo. "A lot of fun. Especially doing it together."

"And the celebration when we finish will be even grander," Mary Jo said.

"Oh, I think we should practice that tonight, don't you?"

"I do," Mary Jo said. "I love practicing celebrating."

They both laughed at that.

And Jean didn't mind that they didn't make it to the hot tub for Mary Jo's final night in town.

She didn't mind at all.

PART SIX
The Plan in Action

CHAPTER TWENTY-THREE

MARY JO WATCHED from her apartment window as Stanton Cobble the Third, a tall, thin man with two bodyguards, pulled up in front of his condo in his limo. Her apartment seemed almost bare and had no personal touches. She really hadn't mentally lived here at all, just used the place as an address and temporary base.

Over the last three months, Mary Jo had watched the man's every move, often from this very window.

And Jean had tracked every move of the man's family as well.

It had turned out that Jean had only taken a few weeks to sell her house and move to the city. And after that, every night, after their target and his family settled in for the night, they met for dinner and wonderful evenings together in Jean's apartment.

So the time apart they had both feared had been short and now Mary Jo was stunned at how well they worked together, adjusting the plan slightly as they learned more and more about their target.

Good old Stanton had shorted them both three million. By the time this was over, he was going to wish he had paid the six million thirty times over. And Mary Jo loved that. Over the last three months of watching the target, she had come to hate him more and more.

Unlike her last target, the sheriff, she could never care for good old Stanton. The guy was just an animal, and actually, it made her mad that he had hired her and Jean to kill the sheriff. Not because he had been her husband, but because her husband had been just a nice man.

But Stanton's money had talked and soon Stanton was going to wish his money had talked a lot louder.

Mary Jo watched as Stanton helped a young woman out of the black stretch limo and past the doorman for the building condo, laughing as they went.

The woman was barely old enough to be legal in Manhattan and had long blonde hair, just as all of Stanton's flings had. If nothing else, the man was predictable in his affairs with younger women.

It would not have surprised Mary Jo or Jean in the slightest if Stanton's wife knew about this secret condo as well and just looked the other way because of the kids and the money and their beautiful apartment overlooking Central Park.

Mary Jo had seen that a great deal over the years as well.

And it disgusted both her and Jean. How could a woman let herself be used like that?

Mary Jo waited until it was clear that good old Stanton was in his condo, then nodded.

The plan was set. Today was the day.

Finally, they were moving.

She quickly checked the cell phone she had for calls from Jean.

Nothing.

The plan was in motion.

Mary Jo closed the window in her apartment across from Stanton's private condo and pulled down the blinds.

She had given notice on this apartment and when she walked out the door shortly she would be done with it.

In four or five months or so, she and Jean hoped to buy Stanton's condo across the street in a fire sale. They would, of course, buy it under a brand new name, not even the fake one she had used in the apartment renting.

She and Jean could afford to live anywhere, but they both thought it might be fun to take over Stanton's love nest after he was long gone.

Besides, this was a great neighborhood and had some fantastic restaurants within walking distance.

It was a perfect neighborhood for her and Jean to live.

And Stanton's condo had one major feature they both loved and had stood beside a number of times in their scouting and planning trips. The condo had a large hot tub overlooking a private roof garden.

Besides that, at two bedrooms, Stanton's condo had a wonderful penthouse view and a kitchen that would make a magazine about top kitchens. They both had decided that living there for a time sure wouldn't be an issue or a hardship on either of them.

Besides, Mary Jo liked the city and she had come to discover that Jean did as well.

"More than anywhere else in the world," Jean had said.

And both of them had lived almost everywhere in the world. But both of them had always found themselves back in New York City.

They talked often about their times in the city, trying to figure out if they had come close to crossing paths at times. They had even taken walks past old apartments, learning each other's history with the city.

Mary Jo was convinced that she would have noticed Jean if their paths had crossed.

Jean had said the same thing about Mary Jo.

Now they were a couple that turned heads.

Jean had said it was because of Mary Jo's beauty. But Mary Jo knew better. It was all because of Jean, the most beautiful woman Mary Jo had ever seen or been with.

And after today, they would have even more time together, at least until their next job.

CHAPTER TWENTY-FOUR

JEAN TOOK A slow walk through the apartment near Stanton's home apartment overlooking Central Park, just making sure nothing was out of place.

Then she quickly checked her phone for a call from Mary Jo.

Nothing.

The plan was a go.

She loved this part of any plan. She never felt worried or bothered by her killing. It was what she did.

What Mary Jo did.

And both of them were very good at their job. But this target felt like something special today. They had no intention of killing him or taking him out in any easy way.

But they were going to end his life in so many other ways.

While Stanton had been getting lax in not worrying about anyone coming for him, Jean and Mary Jo had been exploring every detail of his life, his wife's life, his two kid's lives, his parent's lives, and his businesses and bank accounts.

And the more she and Mary Jo found out, the more angry Jean got at the idiot.

Their fees might have stung the bastard for a few days, but he could have easily paid it. He was just a greedy pile of walking crap.

Now Stanton was going to pay a much, much higher price than the six million he shorted them.

And Jean and Mary Jo were going to be far, far richer.

Over the last six months, to start with, she and Mary Jo had been slowly buying up, under various hidden names, stock in his two publicly held corporations. Stanton was the president of both of them and major stockholder.

In the last week, they had both, also under the hidden names, started selling puts on the stocks they owned, betting that the stocks would fall through the floor.

Because of what they were about to do, Jean had no doubt those two company stocks would quickly vanish from the stock market. And she and Mary Jo would get even richer as it happened.

Mary Jo had great skills with computers, but they had discovered that Jean was even better, which Mary Jo had seemed very pleased about.

With a little work, but frighteningly not that much, Jean had managed to get all Stanton's passwords and bank account numbers, including his two off-the-books accounts.

All told, transferring all his money from those accounts to hidden offshore accounts and then moving it around like scrambling up cards would get her and Mary Jo another six hundred million.

And she had all the corporations' bank account numbers and passwords as well. That would get the two of them another five or six hundred million.

Granted, before this, they both had more than enough money for anything they ever needed. But now they would have even more. All because Stanton was greedy and didn't pay them after he had hired them.

Jean went to the fridge of the apartment and pulled out a pitcher of orange juice and some chilled vodka and filled a tall glass with ice.

Now Available
**from all your favorite booksellers
in trade paper and electronic editions**.

Then with the drink in her hand, she sat on her couch and turned on the television. They had worked in time in the plan for her to watch her favorite soap opera. She loved doing that while sipping on a drink.

This would be the last drink until the job was completely done later tonight, so she was going to savor it.

And then really, really enjoy the drink with Mary Jo later.

CHAPTER TWENTY-FIVE

STANTON'S PARENTS WERE the country club types. They had a huge mansion in the Hamptons and loved being retired there. Stanton paid for it all.

And the two of them were creatures of extreme habit, just as their son. Last night, late, Jean had set a very, very powerful bomb in the Mercedes they always drove to the country club for their afternoon tennis lessons.

Mary Jo wondered if Stanton knew that his parents then paid the tennis pro a very large bonus to have sex with Stanton's mother while his father watched, sucking his thumb.

More than likely not.

When Mary Jo had told Jean about that discovery, she had just shaken her head. "For a change I think we are doing the world a favor here."

"Now don't go getting all superhero on me," Mary Jo had said, smiling at the beautiful face of the woman she loved.

Jean had laughed and later that night had pulled a sheet up over her shoulders, standing naked over Mary Jo in a wonderful position straddling her.

Then Jean had said, "Super Assassin to the rescue."

"I know what will stop Super Assassin," Mary Jo had said.

"Nothing can stop me!" Jean had said.

Mary Jo sat up and buried her face in Jean's crotch, holding her tight by her butt cheeks.

"Well, that will certainly slow a hero down," Jean had said after a long moan.

Mary Jo locked up the apartment after one last check and put her keys in the landlord's mailbox with a thank-you note. Then with just a backpack, she left the building. She had moved what few clothes she had kept there out of the apartment yesterday and given them away to a charity.

Jean would be doing the same thing in their other apartment near Stanton's home shortly. Right after she finished watching her favorite soap opera.

Mary Jo loved the fact that Jean had a favorite soap opera. It didn't interest Mary Jo much, but she loved that Jean was passionate about it.

Two blocks up the street, Mary Jo hailed a cab and was dropped off along the edge of Central Park within a few blocks of Stanton's large apartment looking out over the park.

There, sitting on a park bench so she could see the large apartment balcony, she had her laptop open like any writer out working on a story on a nice afternoon.

She glanced at the time and then she started the ball rolling.

It was exactly three-fifteen in the afternoon.

First, she drained every dollar of both corporation accounts, making the transaction look as if Stanton had taken the money in all respects.

She made the transaction look like it started from his personal laptop computer and then she started the international programs that would make the money completely vanish after dozens of transfers through holding and shell accounts around the world, ending up eventually in one of hers or Jean's many accounts.

Then she did the same with every one of Stanton's bank accounts, making it look like he had transferred all his money offshore. She cashed out everything he had.

She even drained every one of his credit cards.

In just minutes Stanton had gone from having hundreds of millions to not having a dime.

She had also purchased with one of his last credit cards in his name and some phony woman's name, ten different plane tickets for this evening from three different New York area airports to countries that did not extradite.

To anyone, it looked like he had cleaned out everything and was fleeing the country.

There could be no other way anyone could read what had happened, no matter how much Stanton claimed otherwise.

Then, at twenty-nine minutes after the hour, she clicked on a camera link that Jean had hacked into on a camera on a pole in the Hamptons.

Mary Jo knew that Jean would also be watching now, since her soap was over.

The Hamptons had great security cameras. But the security system was far too easy to hack into to be worthwhile. It was how Jean had gotten in and out undetected to plant the bomb.

As Mary Jo watched, Stanton's parents, all dressed up in their tennis outfits, came out of the back door of the house as the garage door opened.

They climbed into their Mercedes.

A few seconds later the camera flashed and when the image cleared, it showed most of the house completely destroyed and in flames. Debris was flying through the air.

"Boom," Mary Jo said.

Then she destroyed that link.

Stanton Cobble the Third was just starting to pay.

CHAPTER TWENTY-SIX

JEAN WATCHED ON her laptop in her apartment as Stanton's parents were removed from the planet by the bomb she had planted. She had used enough explosives to take out half of the house just in case one of them hadn't been inside the car.

They both had been, so the police would be scraping pieces of those two out of the surrounding neighborhood for a month.

Jean deleted any evidence of the link and clicked into a second link. She knew that Mary Jo was watching the same thing she was. That made her happy, actually. She never had been able to share her passion, her work with anyone before.

Jean shut off the television, put her glass in the sink for someone to wash later, then moved to the window and opened the blinds before going back to the couch. She knew that Mary Jo had a front row seat in the park somewhere. Jean was going to get the front row seat here because she could see Stanton's apartment clearly out of a side front room window.

She had spent a lot of time in Stanton's apartment, actually, exploring every nook and cranny. It was a beautiful place, worth the millions it cost him.

Or it would be for a short time.

A very short time.

Stanton's wife was also a creature of extreme habit. The kids did not get home until four in the afternoon, so at three-thirty, Stanton's wife always took a shower.

Jean watched the feed of the bathroom door of Stanton's wife's bedroom in their penthouse apartment. After a shower that lasted exactly five minutes, Stanton's wife, a brunette with dyed blonde hair came out of the bathroom with a towel on her head and headed for her closet. The woman had a nice body and kept herself in shape. Too bad Stanton was such an idiot and didn't pay attention.

And too bad the woman let Stanton be such a bastard. Staying with someone just for the money was never worth the price it cost, in Jean's opinion.

Stanton's wife was going to pay a very heavy price for what her husband had done.

Jean pushed three keys at the same time on her laptop.

A moment later, the camera link flashed and went dead.

Jean looked up to see the explosion shattering the entire top of the building, making people on the sidewalk below flee in panic from all the falling debris.

"Boom," Jean said a fraction of a second before the sound of the real explosion reached her.

Stanton had now lost his wife, his parents, and every penny he had.

And he would be quickly arrested, since she and Mary Jo had tipped off a number of police, the FBI, and the Security and Exchange commission about Stanton and his plans to skip town.

His children would be without money and would end up living with his wife's parents, two nice people outside of Chicago. More than likely they would be better off with their grandparents than living with Stanton.

Jean watched the cloud of smoke rise up into the air over the large penthouse. She didn't even smile.

Stanton should have paid Jean and Mary Jo their final fee.

It really was that simple.

Jean closed her laptop, put it in a backpack, checked the apartment one more time and headed for the door, leaving the keys on the dresser for the landlord to find.

She had a dinner date with a beautiful woman and she needed to get ready.

CHAPTER TWENTY-SEVEN

MARY JO GOT to their new apartment just a minute before Jean did. They kissed and hugged and then both laughed.

Their apartment together was about ten blocks from Stanton's lover's nest and was also a penthouse, but it didn't have a hot tub and they both missed that.

They spent the next hour on Jean's computer, making sure all the money had moved correctly and was now impossible to trace and living in their accounts.

Mary Jo wasn't even surprised at how much richer she and Jean both were now.

It made no difference to her, since they hadn't done this for the money. But it still pleased her.

In her world, money and death were staples of what she worked for.

And now she lived for Jean and for a good vodka and orange juice.

After dealing with the money, they both got dressed up and headed out for a wonderful night on the town. They had a perfect dinner followed by a little dancing at a local club and then some wonderful lovemaking after they got home.

And, there was vodka and orange juice involved all along the way.

The next morning, Mary Jo awoke smelling rich coffee and eggs.

She washed her face, put on her bathrobe and joined Jean in the kitchen.

The television was on low, but loud enough to hear.

"Anything happening in the world?" Mary Jo asked.

Jean came over and kissed her, poured her a cup of coffee, and then went back to fixing the eggs.

"The press is saying some rich businessman blew up his wife and his parents," Jean said, "so he could escape with his bimbo. It wasn't terrorists at all."

"That's good to know it wasn't terrorists," Mary Jo said. "Did they catch him?"

"They got him coming out of a love nest not far from here."

"Perfect," Mary Jo said, laughing. "Couldn't have happened to a nicer man."

"Got that right," Jean said.

They ate and laughed and talked and Mary Jo knew that wonderful breakfast was the start of their new life together.

Then, two months later, on the anniversary of what they called The Event, when Mary Jo killed both Jean's and her own husband, Mary Jo and Jean put a bid in on Stanton's love nest. A bid so high, they knew they would get it.

After all, they were using Stanton's own money.

Then at exactly three-ten in the afternoon, while standing on the sidewalk outside what they hoped would be their new condo, they used a burner phone to put in a call to Stanton where he was being held on suicide watch in a prison upstate.

Mary Jo had sent money through channels to make sure one of the guards gave Stanton a burner phone as well at exactly the right time.

And she gave the guard enough money also for after the phone call, to make Stanton hurt a little without killing him.

Mary Jo stood close to Jean against a stone wall of one building, holding the phone out on speaker so Jean could hear.

"Yes," Stanton said.

The sound of Stanton's voice just made Mary Jo shudder.

"You should have paid us the six million," Mary Jo said.

Then she clicked off the phone and dropped it into a bag of bagels she had just bought. Then ten steps later she dropped the entire bag into a garbage can. She had rigged the phone to melt into a pool in two minutes after she used it.

Then the two of them walked hand-in-hand back toward their penthouse.

"Wow, that felt wonderful," Jean said. "Just flat wonderful."

Mary Jo had to agree. It did feel fantastic. Usually killing a target didn't feel this good. But they hadn't actually killed their target.

At least not in a way that would make it easy on him.

But they had made sure he knew who had done all this to him. And having him know felt perfect.

Three months later, she and Jean were looking over the empty condo and the recently cleaned hot tub of Stanton's former love nest. They had just bought the place and the two of them were planning furniture and acting like excited schoolgirls getting ready for the first day of school, especially around the wonderful rooftop hot tub.

Mary Jo loved the city.

Mary Jo loved Jean.

And they both loved the condo.

And surprisingly also important, Mary Jo had realized that she loved vodka and orange juice even more when she had someone to enjoy it with.

PART SEVEN
A Disturbance

CHAPTER TWENTY-EIGHT

THEY HAD A stalker.

Mary Jo needed to tell Jean. But she didn't want to. She knew what she had to say would change everything.

And the last year had been wonderful. They even had planned a night on the town for the second anniversary of The Event. Mary Jo had never imagined herself being so happy, so content with a life.

Both of them in the last year had turned down offers for targets. Both of them just wanted to enjoy the time for as long as they could.

SMITH'S Monthly

But Mary Jo had no doubt what she had seen would change that and change everything.

So that morning, while they were both eating a light breakfast of eggs and toast around their small, but cozy, kitchen table that looked out at the rooftop garden, Mary Jo just blurted it out.

"We're being followed. Maybe targeted."

Jean glanced up from her iPad, her toast halfway to her mouth. Mary Jo could see instant worry in Jean's wonderful green eyes.

"It's a pro, I'm sure," Mary Jo said. "Maybe from the order."

"Why would anyone hire an assassin against one of us?" Jean asked.

Mary Jo shook her head. "I have no idea. Maybe our last client decided to finish the job before we finished him and the assassin was never called off. You know how patient we can all be."

Jean put her toast down and sat back, staring at Mary Jo with her intense green eyes.

Mary Jo hated to ruin such a perfectly good day, but they had to work together now to solve whatever was happening. That was one of the hardest things Mary Jo was trying to adapt to, that there was two of them now. She had a partner and she actually loved that fact, something she never would have thought possible before.

"Describe what you saw, exactly," Jean said.

Mary Jo nodded and went carefully through the details of spotting the stalker three different times. The woman following them was as short as they were, with short black hair and a dark skin. The woman had all the traits of an assassin of the order.

Jean listened until Mary Jo was done, then said simply, "I've seen her as well. But didn't realize she was following us. Very good observation."

That shocked and worried Mary Jo even more.

"You ever targeted another order member?" Jean asked. "I haven't."

Two Earth Protection League Stories
Available at your favorite booksellers.

Mary Jo shook her head. "Never. Can't imagine it ever happening."

Jean nodded. "So first we find out if this person following us is an order member."

Mary Jo watched as Jean stood and vanished into the side room where she kept what little personal things she had kept from their last job. She came back a moment later.

Mary Jo couldn't imagine calling the order for anything, but clearly Jean didn't have that problem at all. Mary Jo had a phone with a direct link to the order just as Jean did, but she always kept it turned off and in a heavy metal box.

Jean smiled, but the smile didn't reach her green eyes. Then she punched one key.

After a tense moment of silence she said, "Freyia Mist."

Mary Jo knew that was Jean's order name. Mary Jo's order name at the moment was Angela Sea. It had been numbers of others over the centuries.

"I am with another order member," Jean said into the phone. "Angela Sea. Are we being targeted by an order member?"

Jean listened for a moment, then said simply, "Understood."

She hung up and put the phone on the table.

Mary Jo just sat, waiting as Jean took a deep breath.

"We are not being targeted by another order member and it is against order rules for one member to turn on another for any reason."

Mary Jo felt a huge sense of relief.

"Thank you," she said to Jean.

"So any suggestions?" Jean asked, smiling and this time the smile reached her eyes.

"Now that we know that critical fact," Mary Jo said, "I think we need to invite our stalker to the party."

"We're throwing a party?"

"I think we should," Mary Jo said, smiling. "A very intimate party with just you and me and our stalker."

Jean laughed. "Think she'll like vodka and orange juice?"

"If not," Mary Jo said, "she won't be allowed to stay."

CHAPTER TWENTY-NINE

THE FALL DAY was perfect in the city, with temperatures just over sixty and a slight breeze. The trees in the city hadn't started losing their leaves yet, but Jean had no doubt it wouldn't be long now.

Today, she was in disguise. She had on a red-haired wig and wore older jeans and a T-shirt with a denim jacket. She would never go out like this normally, but today she and Mary Jo had what they called "Invite Day." Their stalker was going to join them even if she didn't want to.

After that morning, they had double-checked their condo's security for any unwanted bugs and also checked other apartments for line-of-sight watching, just as Mary Jo had done when good old Stanton had used this condo to meet his mistress.

They found nothing, so their stalker was depending on following them in routines.

This morning Jean had gone out the back in the dark and circled around to where they had a Jeep SUV parked two blocks from their condo. Jean moved the SUV into position and then left it.

Mary Jo's morning routine three days a week was to walk along this street to the market, do some shopping and then carry the groceries back. She liked getting out and meeting people, while Jean had her groceries delivered for the meals she cooked.

Jean sat on the ground in a recessed doorway, hidden, as Mary Jo walked by right on time.

As she did, Mary Jo touched her hair on the right side, indicating the stalker was behind her. The plan was for Mary Jo to go another half block, let the stalker get past Jean, then turn suddenly and start back, as if forgetting something.

Jean was going to be interested in seeing how the stalker woman reacted when that happened.

Jean kept her head down enough for the hair to cover most of her face and make it look as if she was a junkie sleeping. But with one eye she could see the street and those passing by.

Following Mary Jo at about one block distance, the stalker passed.

Jean had out her small pistol that contained a dart with enough drug to stop a horse in its tracks.

She stood and stepped into the street just behind the stalker, keeping the pistol hidden.

The woman was dressed in jeans, tennis shoes, and a very fashionable blouse that Jean could see the sports bra under. Her pitch-black hair almost shone in the morning sun and her face looked freshly scrubbed and radiant.

The woman was a stunner, of that there was no doubt. Jean hoped they didn't have to kill her. It would be such a waste of beauty.

The stalker also had the walk of a member of the order. Even though she was just strolling down the sidewalk, Jean could tell she made not one sound.

Suddenly one block ahead, Mary Jo turned and started back, as if she had forgotten something.

The stalker did exactly as Jean would have done. She just kept walking at Mary Jo. The stalker was going to be looking at something else purposely when she passed Mary Jo.

There was no sign of the stalker carrying a weapon, but that didn't mean she didn't have one.

As Mary Jo got ten paces away, Jean put the dart into the beautiful skin of the stalker's neck, right above her blouse collar.

The stalker spun instantly, seeing Jean, but at that point the stalker was already heading for the ground.

Mary Jo caught her and lowered her down on the edge of the sidewalk, out of the path of others.

Jean joined her.

"Looks like she fainted," Mary Jo said, pretending to check the woman's pulse and breathing while making sure the dart in the woman's neck vanished from sight.

"What do we do?" Jean asked, playing her part in the little drama play.

"We need to get her to a hospital," Mary Jo said. "Her heart is beating irregularly."

Around them a group of five or six had gathered. Jean was paying close attention to all of them in case the woman had a partner. The lookers all seemed to be just lookers.

"I've got a car right here," Jean said, playing the script they had planned for the broad daylight takedown. "I'll drive you. We can have here there in minutes."

Mary Jo nodded, being very serious. "Thank you."

Mary Jo picked up the woman and Jean ran ahead and got the back door to the SUV open.

No one on the sidewalk objected, but instead just nodded at how two good Samaritans were taking care of the poor woman who had passed out on the sidewalk.

Mary Jo got into the back seat with the woman while Jean ran around and got behind the wheel.

Four minutes later they had circled around and were down into the underground parking under their condo building.

And ten minutes later they had the woman on their spare bed in their penthouse condo.

Jean was amazed at how she and Mary Jo worked together so easily to make something very difficult seem almost simple. She liked being Mary Jo's partner.

And she liked having her as a friend and a lover even more.

CHAPTER THIRTY

MARY JO SAT in a desk chair across the room from the black-haired woman. They had brought her into the apartment, stripped her and found no weapons, put her underwear back on and then put zipties on her hands and legs. She was on the bed in their guest room, looking almost radiant against the tan spread.

Sun from the one window in the room beamed through the closed blinds, warming the room a little.

As a trained assassin, the woman was still dangerous, but Mary Jo wasn't worried about her at all. If she had wanted them dead, chances are they would already be dead.

No, this woman had allowed herself to be seen for some reason and Mary Jo was dying to find out why.

"Awake yet," Jean asked as she came into the room and handed Mary Jo a screwdriver, then took the other chair facing the bed.

"Yeah, she's been awake for about ten minutes now, but pretending to still be out."

"Tricky," Jean said.

"Why did you take me?" the woman on the bed asked, opening her eyes and staring first at Jean, then at Mary Jo.

Mary Jo was stunned at the intensity of the woman's dark eyes. She was built almost exactly the same as Mary Jo and Jean, but seemed to have an energy that felt slightly different.

Independent, actually, and a little feeling of being a trapped animal. Mary Jo wouldn't have liked being tied up as she was either.

"She speaks," Jean said, tipping her glass in a toast to Mary Jo.

"Why were you shadowing us?" Mary Jo asked.

"You would not believe me if I told you," the woman said.

"Give us a try," Jean said. "Amazing what we might believe."

"I wanted to ask for your help."

Mary Jo glanced at Jean, then back at the woman on the bed. Of all the things she might have said, that wasn't one that Mary Jo had expected.

"Start at the beginning," Jean said, sitting forward. "Your name and your order name."

"I go by Susan at the moment. My order name is Leila Dark."

Jean nodded and stood. "I'll check with the order to make sure you exist."

Jean left and the woman looked at Mary Jo. "She talks with the order?"

"She does," Mary Jo said, smiling.

"I was hoping she would," Susan said. "Even though I seldom do."

Mary Jo said nothing. She sat sipping her screwdriver in silence as the two waited for Jean to return.

Mary Jo didn't know what to think of this assassin they had captured. But at the moment Mary Jo wasn't getting a bad feeling about Susan. And since no one had paid to target either Mary Jo or Jean, there had to be another reason Susan had shown herself as she did.

Jean came back into the room after just a minute, walked across the room to the bed and sliced the bindings, then returned to sit next to Mary Jo, taking another sip of her drink as she did.

"She checks out with the order," Jean said.

Susan sat up in the bed and put her back against the wall, propping herself up with a pillow but not bothering to ask for her clothes.

Mary Jo wouldn't have either in Susan's position.

"I assume," Mary Jo said, "that you let us see you so you would get this meeting. Correct?"

Susan nodded.

"Took a chance we wouldn't kill you," Jean said.

"No order assassin kills without cause and you had no cause with me," Susan said.

"She has a point," Mary Jo said. "But you could have just knocked on our door and introduced yourself."

"No fun in that," Susan said, smiling. "But besides, I still wasn't sure you two were who I was looking for. It is not often you find two assassins living together."

Jean shook her head and Mary Jo decided right then that she was going to like this woman.

"So how did you find us, first off?" Jean asked.

"I have been looking for you, Mary Jo," Susan said, "for almost three years."

Mary Jo was stunned at that. She started to ask why, but Susan held up her hand so she could finish her story.

"When I heard about the killings in the northern part of the state, I knew that had the markings of an assassin. So I started looking at the victims and it became clear that your target had been the sheriff. He was the only one who made sense out of all the ones who died, including the writer."

Mary Jo was impressed.

Susan went on. "So I next researched the sheriff's wife and the other victim's families first. Learned about both of you, but honestly didn't suspect either of you at that point."

"Good to know," Jean said.

Susan nodded. "Then I backtracked who would have hired any assassin to kill the sheriff and found a piece of trash named Stanton Cobble the Third. So I staked him out until I noticed the sheriff's wife also staking him out. I wasn't surprised when I discovered it was you, Mary Jo. That hit on the sheriff was so perfectly done."

Mary Jo nodded and let Susan continue. But it wasn't often an assassin got complimented on a job. In fact, for Mary Jo, that was the first time in centuries.

"And then I was even more surprised," Susan said, "to find that Jean was also helping. So I figured the idiot Stanton had hired two assassins for the job and then shorted you both. Right?"

"Got that exactly," Jean said.

"I loved what you both did to Stanton," Susan said. "Elegant. Completely elegant. It was a joy to watch."

"Thank you," Jean said, smiling.

Mary Jo toasted Susan and nodded her thanks as well. But the story still hadn't gotten to why this woman had been looking for years for Mary Jo. And what help did she need.

"So for the last year I stayed out of sight, occasionally tracking your movements. Finally, this last week I decided it was time to show myself. I am running out of time, it seems."

"Time for what?" Mary Jo asked.

"Time to kill my target," Susan said. "What else?"

With that, the three of them just sat there in silence.

And Mary Jo was more confused now than she had been when Susan started her story.

And that was going some.

CHAPTER THIRTY-ONE

JEAN STARED AT the beautiful assassin sitting on their guest bed. She had just told them a story that seemed clear and logical and very clean of problems. That bothered Jean a little, but not that much.

What bothered Jean was that the assassin was looking for help to kill a target. That meant the target was almost impossible to kill. A sniper's bullet could take down a target from a distance and over the

---

Some Classic Dean Wesley Smith Stories
Available at your favorite booksellers.

centuries, Jean had used that method on targets she couldn't get close to.

Jean was sure that Susan had as well.

"You've been looking for me for three years to help you with a target?" Mary Jo said. "Why me, first off?"

"You are known for being the best of us all," Susan said flatly.

Jean nodded and turned to her partner and roommate, who was looking surprised. "You do have that reputation."

Jean watched as Mary Jo just shook her head and clearly ignored that line of thinking.

"Why is this target so difficult?" Mary Jo asked.

"Because," Susan said, "he's supposed to be already dead. He might be for all I know at the moment."

Silence filled the room among the three assassins.

Jean felt even more confused, but before she could ask her next question, Mary Jo did.

"Already dead, meaning in deep hiding?" Mary Jo asked. "Or doesn't exist as in a fictional construct?"

"Yes, yes, and also," Susan said, clearly pained by what she was about to say, "the target is supposed to return from the dead in one year."

"He's in deep hiding, fictional, and a religious figure?" Jean asked.

Susan nodded, clearly pained at that response.

"Real tough to kill if the target is already dead," Mary Jo said, sipping on her screwdriver.

"Now you see my problem," Susan said.

Jean wasn't sure what she saw. She needed a lot more information and getting that information was going to take time.

"Why don't you get dressed," Jean said, standing and indicating that she wanted to talk with Mary Jo for a moment. "Then join us in the kitchen."

"Thank you for even considering this," Susan said, nodding. "I've pretty much run out of ideas and options."

"I can imagine," Mary Jo said, shaking her head and standing.

Then Jean led the way out of the guest room and into the kitchen area.

"Is she nuts, playing us, or in real need of help?" Jean asked softly as they reached their kitchen. She loved the kitchen area of the condo because it had modern appliances and a wonderful eating nook looking out over a roof garden and the neighborhood beyond.

"Need of help," Mary Jo said, sitting at the table and taking another sip of her screwdriver. "She seems as sane as either one of us, approached us perfectly, and I can see of no reason she would play us. No gain."

"Agree," Jean said. "So you want to help her?"

"I want to hear more," Mary Jo said. "But if we decide to help her, I think she should move in here for a short time with us. Until we take down the target."

Jean nodded. "I had thought the same thing."

"So you still cooking tonight or you want me to?"

Jean smiled. "I'd love to cook and I have enough for three without a problem."

She liked the idea of cooking for the three of them. That alone made her happy.

"Perfect," Mary Jo said, smiling. "Let's go for lunch down to Steven's Deli and talk there for a time, then come back here for more talking and dinner. How does that sound?"

"Planning a target strike is always fun," Jean said, smiling.

Mary Jo smiled and made a toasting motion with her glass. "My targets always end up dead. Never had one already dead before."

Jean had to drink to that as well. There was no doubt the day had turned interesting.

No doubt at all.

CHAPTER THIRTY-TWO

MARY JO SAT directly across a small Formica tabletop from Susan and next to Jean at a window table in Steven's Deli. The deli was small and had only ten tables and a long meat and sandwich counter. A wall of windows along one wall made the place feel like it was almost open to the city street.

Only two construction workers at a back table were in the place at the moment.

Mary Jo loved it here, since not only did they make a great salad with radishes and cucumbers and carrots, but the corned beef was some of the best in the city and that was going some for New York.

Besides that, the place always smelled heavenly of fresh bread and roasting meat combined.

Just on the other side of the wall of windows the normally busy traffic of New York streamed past. A delivery truck sat half onto the sidewalk near the back of the deli so that it forced people on the sidewalk into single-file along the windows.

Mary Jo loved how not a person walking by seemed to mind. It was just all part of a day in the city.

All three of them were eating basically the same lunch. All three had salads and

Jean used an Italian dressing while Susan and Mary Jo both used vinegar and oil with a little salt. All three drank from bottles of water.

It turned out Susan came here often as well and the owner behind the counter had even called her by name when they came in. You had to be a regular in New York before that started happening.

And that meant that Susan lived somewhere in this neighborhood as well.

After they got seated, Mary Jo put a small phone-sized device on the table among them and clicked it on. "That blocks anyone listening to or recording this conversation from anywhere around us."

Susan nodded and didn't seem concerned in the slightest.

"So back to the beginning," Jean said.

"You are going to have to confide everything in us," Mary Jo said. "I know that's not something we normally do in the order, but if we're going to help you, we need to know every detail."

Susan nodded again. "I had planned on that when I started searching for you for help."

Silence except for the two construction workers across the small deli talking about some football game that Mary Jo didn't care about.

Susan took another bite of her salad and then started into her story. Mary Jo couldn't imagine telling anyone about her getting hired for a target and all the preliminary stuff she did, but they needed to know it all from Susan.

"I was contracted six years ago to target a man by the name of Jack Kelsall."

Mary Jo glanced at Jean to see if she recognized the name. Clearly she didn't.

"I was offered three million up front and seven million if I completed the task in a public fashion."

"Wow," Jean said. "Way above order normal."

Mary Jo nodded. She had never heard of any assassin being offered that kind of money before. She had never come close to that amount, actually.

"The money doesn't matter to me anymore," Susan said. "Just part of the job. But I took the job and told the client it would take a lot of time. They gave me seven years."

"Why seven years?" Mary Jo asked. There seemed to be no logical reason for such a time period.

"Seven years from the time I was hired," Susan said, "Jack Kelsall will rise from the dead and speak to his followers and lead them into the new world, or some such garbage like that. Mostly he'll just take a lot more of their money."

"A dead guy has followers?" Jean asked a half second before Mary Jo could ask the same question.

"Millions and millions of them," Susan said. "More by the day now. All waiting for him to rise from the dead. If he does, it will be sensational beyond words, a long con that took twenty-five years to set up and play out."

Susan had been talking and all Mary Jo had gotten was more confused.

"I am missing some huge bits of information here," Mary Jo said and beside her Jean was nodding her head as well. "Explain what you mean by a long con?"

"Twenty-five years ago," Susan said, "Jack Kelsall and a close friend by the name of Carson White started a small religion based on the belief that it was possible to return from death to become immortal. Both were archeology and history students so they actually took some truths from our ancient order beliefs, but got most wrong."

"Okay," Mary Jo said. She didn't want to sidetrack the conversation by digging into order beliefs that had made the three of them basically immortal. That would be a conversation for later.

"The religion they set up is called Ever Life. It had managed to attract enough followers to make a little money with their scam. But they needed to have Kelsall die and then come back to life to make the big bucks in the con."

"So that's what's behind Ever Life," Jean said, shaking her head. "Always wondered."

"Never heard of it before," Mary Jo said.

"You are lucky," Susan said. "They seem to be everywhere these days as the promised resurrection gets closer."

"So Kelsall faked his own death and went into hiding twenty-four years ago," Mary Jo said, starting to understand the problem a little better.

"And Carson White kept running the church," Jean said.

Susan nodded. "They faked a jump from a bridge, body never found. Then White and the remaining church members got to work on Jack's promise to return to his congregation in exactly twenty-five years, an immortal being."

"And they've been milking these poor souls for money the entire time?" Jean asked.

"They have," Susan said. "Thousands of prep products, courses to learn balance and rituals to prepare the soul to leave and then return as an immortal being. All costing thousands and thousands. They have taken in more millions than I want to imagine."

"A real long con," Mary Jo said. "Just like any typical religion."

Jean nodded to that.

Mary Jo sat there in silence as the other two kept eating. This was really an amazing scam this guy was pulling. Amazing and about to work unless they found and really put the guy into the ground first.

In a public fashion.

And if three order assassins couldn't do that, working together, no one could.

CHAPTER THIRTY-THREE

JEAN CONTINUED TO work on her salad as Susan filled in some details about the target. It seemed Kelsall had loved the finer things in life, had no real family to speak of, and at least before his death had never been married.

In fact, other than a degree from the University of Wisconsin Madison, and his friendship with another student, Carson White, Kelsall seemed to have a very unremarkable life until he and White decided to start their own religion.

"I got pictures and backgrounds on both of them," Susan said. "And every bit of data I have dug up on them and their church I'll be glad to show you, including the film taken of Kelsall making his jump from the Golden Gate Bridge."

"Long distance images I'll bet," Mary Jo said.

Susan shook her head, which stopped Jean in mid-bite.

"Close-up from three different angles on the bridge from three different stationary cameras of him going off the side," Jean said. "Then two long-shots of his fall and hitting the water, one from each bank."

"Got any idea how they faked that?" Mary Jo asked.

Susan nodded. "Had Kelsall stand on the edge of the bridge just over a net strung from the side of the bridge. He jumped into the net. Then they cleared the net and filmed a dummy going over from a distance, weighted so it looked like a human body falling. It would be heavy enough to sink and quickly dissolve in the water."

"Real enough that no one would question it," Jean said. She was amazed at the skill that had taken to plan.

"What they are not questioning," Mary Jo said, "is the twenty-five years. If he had come back in six months, the questions would be everywhere. The brilliance of this con is the twenty-five years."

"Exactly," Susan said.

Jean nodded to that. Then asked, "So who hired you?"

"A parent of one of the kids trapped in the deeper cult of this fake church," Susan said. "If we can expose this as a fake, my client thinks his kid will be able to walk away."

"More than likely right on that score," Jean said, nodding.

"Even after six years?" Mary Jo asked.

Susan nodded. "My client is afraid that if this guy actually does come back and make it look like he's coming back from the dead, my client's kid will kill herself to try to gain the same immortality."

"So where have you looked for Kelsall?" Jean asked.

"Everywhere," Susan said, the tiredness and hopelessness clear in her voice. "I figured that following the money would be the way to track Kelsall, since he liked to live high, but no money leaves the church. It all just pours in."

"And where does White live?" Mary Jo asked.

"In the church compound," Susan said. "He lives the life of a king, of that there is no doubt, but I can't find any way that money is being filtered to anyone outside the church. And I've done some deep tracking."

"You mind if we double-check you on that?" Mary Jo asked.

"Please," Susan said.

They all finished their lunch with a few more basic questions, then Susan left for her apartment to get what she had dug up in six years of searching while Mary Jo and Jean strolled leisurely back toward their condo.

Jean loved walking with Mary Jo like this. Their strides matched and neither of them minded walking in silence.

This entire thing sure felt odd to Jean. Something was very wrong that Susan, clearly a smart and well-trained guild assassin, couldn't find Kelsall. So finally, about a block from their condo, Jean broke the silence.

"You think Kelsall is alive? Or is this Carson White and his people just milking what they can for as long as they can?"

Mary Jo sort of shrugged. "I'm betting he's still alive and hiding. We just have to figure out where and then figure out how to get him into the open and kill him."

"He's slipped somewhere, right. That is what you are saying?"

Jean smiled at the woman she loved.

Mary Jo smiled back. "Twenty-four years in hiding. He's slipped. We just have to figure out where."

Jean took Mary Jo's hand. "Kind of fun to be back on the chase, isn't it?"

"Tremendous fun," Mary Jo said. "And challenging at the same time."

"The best of both worlds," Jean said.

Mary Jo squeezed her hand in agreement.

CHAPTER THIRTY-FOUR

MARY JO COULDN'T believe how completely thorough Susan had been in her search for Jack Kelsall. Over a week-long period, with the three women eating together and Susan staying with them in the condo, Mary Jo and Jean double- and triple-checked everything Susan had done.

And tried a few other dead-end ideas as well.

They had set up the condo's large dining area with three work stations, all protected from any kind of tracing. And they had covered one wall with a giant war board of print-outs and a twenty-four-year timeline.

Finally, after yet another dead-end idea panned out, Susan sighed and said simply, "I'm starting to believe that Jack Kelsall really died twenty-four years ago."

Mary Jo turned from her work station and stared at the black-haired assassin, an idea slowly starting to form.

"Someone died that day," Mary Jo said. "I've studied that film now a bunch of times and I believe that was a real body dropping off that bridge."

Jean looked at her and Susan stopped and just stared.

Mary Jo stood and went to the files that Susan had accumulated over six years of research that were scattered on the top of the dining room table. She pulled out a college picture of Jack Kelsall standing next to Carson White.

Both boys, not more than nineteen at the time of the picture, were the same height. Both were thin and from their arms draped over each other's shoulders, clearly best friends. Jack had dark hair, Carson's was blond. Jack had a smaller nose. Carson's nose was larger and wider.

Mary Jo looked closer at the picture. She could see that Carson's eyes were blue, Jack's eyes were dark brown.

Jack wore his dark hair long, Carson wore his blond hair cropped short.

The picture was taken about four years before the bridge.

"What are you thinking," Jean asked.

Mary Jo didn't say anything. She honestly wasn't sure what she was thinking. But without Kelsall still alive somewhere, this entire religion was going to go down in flames in exactly one year.

"You got a recent picture of Carson?"

Susan flipped open her iPad and a moment later placed it on the dining table so Mary Jo and Jean could both see the blond-haired man. He was still trim and clearly wore his money well. Same wide nose, same blue eyes.

"He doesn't go out in public very often," Susan said. "Pictures of him are rare. Other than the church, he has no family, never married, stays to himself mostly in his mansion on the church grounds."

"Does he have a girlfriend?" Mary Jo asked, hoping "or a series of them?"

"Boyfriends," Susan said.

Mary Jo liked the sound of that.

"Could that be Jack Kelsall, hiding in plain sight?" Jean asked, staring at the picture.

"As crazy an idea as any," Mary Jo said. "It would explain no money leaving the church."

"So what happened to Carson White?" Susan asked.

"Carson went off the bridge instead of Kelsall," Mary Jo said. "We need to search the morgue records from the time in the entire area for anyone pulled out of the ocean that would match Carson's basic description."

Three Ghost of a Chance Stories
Available at your favorite booksellers.

Without another word, all three of them turned back to their own work stations.

Mary Jo was excited. She always knew when she was on the right track with something and this was the right track.

"I'll take the east bay area," Jean said.

"I have the San Francisco records," Susan said.

"I'll take the north bay towns and the coastal towns where a body might wash up if the tide was going out," Mary Jo said.

It was Susan who found Carson, at least the dead Carson, forty minutes later.

"Got him," Susan said.

Mary Jo could feel a slight jolt of excitement as she and Jean both stood and moved over behind Susan.

"John Doe," Susan read. "Six-foot tall, blond hair, blue eyes, fished out of the bay two days after the jump. Never identified."

Then she glanced around at Mary Jo and Jean, a slight smile on her face. "Cause of death was blunt force trauma to the head. Kelsall smashed in his friend's skull and dumped his body off the bridge."

"Clothes?" Mary Jo asked.

Susan went back to the report, then smiled again, this time even wider. "Same clothes that Kelsall was wearing when he was filmed jumping."

"We found the target," Mary Jo said, smiling. "Hiding as they often do, right in plain sight."

"So now we get to the fun part," Jean said, smiling back at Mary Jo. "How do we expose him and then kill him?"

"Oh, this is going to be such fun," Susan said, clapping her hands together. "Tonight, dinner is on me."

And as far as Mary Jo was concerned, it was a great dinner at one of the neighborhood's nicest steak houses.

And that evening wasn't bad either, back in the hot tub, naked and sipping screwdrivers with two beautiful women.

A memorable night of celebration all around.

PART EIGHT
Setting the Plan

CHAPTER THIRTY-FIVE

JEAN COULD NOT believe the security that the Ever Life Church had built up around their main compound. She and Mary Jo and Susan had taken the next week digging out every detail they could find about the place, including original plans for most of the buildings.

The sixty-acre compound draped over a ridgeline on the edge of the Sierra Mountains, with views out over Sacramento and the San Francisco Bay area in the far distance.

One major two-lane paved road led into the compound, winding up a valley from below. High stone walls and electrical fences on top of the walls surrounded the entire complex.

Jean had seen less security at major prisons.

And clearly there was a vast amount of money in the compound. Over forty homes, a number of what looked like condo complexes, dozens of large halls and other areas, not counting the large mansion that sat on the highest point of the ridge.

The place was a marvel of architecture and art.

The security systems were combinations of electronic, guards on foot, dogs, and a no-mans-land along the edge of the wall on the inside with electrical fences and from what Jean could tell land mines.

Drones patrolled the area outside the walls like a vast swarm of bugs.

The entire compound also worked off the grid, with its own electrical generation plant and wells and sewage facility.

And there didn't seem to be any Internet connection going into that compound. Or at least none that they could find.

After three days of all of them focusing on finding any flaw in the security of the compound, they met at the small kitchen table in the condo. Mary Jo had made a wonderful chicken meal the night before and had saved some of the chicken for sandwiches on fresh bread.

For Jean, the handmade mustard Mary Jo had done made the sandwich heavenly.

"What would make these people get so paranoid as to build this compound?" Susan asked.

"Not a popular religion," Mary Jo said.

"It's a cult and cults have their detractors," Jean said, "like sane parents who would go to all ends to rescue their children."

"So anyone have any idea how we get in there?" Susan asked.

"We don't need to go in," Jean said, smiling.

Mary Jo laughed. "I love it when she gets that twinkle in her eye and that devious smile."

"So how?" Susan asked, smiling as well.

"We take him out from a distance. All three of us."

"Sniper?" Mary Jo asked.

Jean nodded. "From three sides. But we need to flush him out of his mansion and into the open in his compound first. And to do that, we use his own defenses against him."

Mary Jo laughed. "I have no idea what you are thinking, but I sure like the sounds of it."

"How about we go down to Steven's Deli for some cheesecake dessert," Jean said as she pushed her empty plate forward, imaging how wonderful that cheesecake would taste right about now. "And I'll explain the bones of my plan there."

"Perfect," Mary Jo said.

"I sure like how you two think," Susan said, laughing. "Especially over dessert."

At the deli, Mary Jo set up the sound-blocking device so they couldn't be overheard or recorded in any fashion, then Jean laid out her plan.

"Step one is hijacking the drones," Jean said as she cut into her thick piece of cheesecake with a fork.

"Override their frequencies," Mary Jo said, nodding.

"No need to override them," Jean said after letting the first bite of the cheesecake melt in her mouth for a moment. "Just short them out or block them completely. Basically just shut them off."

"They would fall out of the sky like dead birds," Susan said, nodding.

"But that's not going to flush him out of his mansion," Mary Jo said. "That might put him deeper in hiding, actually. Which reminds me, we need to triple check for hidden escape tunnels as well."

"Already checked for them twice," Susan said.

"I did the same," Jean said after another bite of the wonderful cheesecake. It was so good, it made her mouth water between bites. "But I'm betting they are there and we haven't spotted them yet."

"So you got an idea on how to get him out into the open?" Mary Jo asked, smiling at Jean.

Jean loved that smile, loved everything about Mary Jo, actually.

"I got a hunch that our target will come out of his house if Jack Kelsall walks up to the gate."

Both Mary Jo and Susan stared at her for a moment, then started laughing.

Jean had a hunch that meant they both really liked her plan.

CHAPTER THIRTY-SIX

MARY JO LOVED Jean's idea for flushing Jack Kelsall out of his mansion. Having Jack return from the dead months early would be something, of that there would be no doubt.

But there were problems with the plan. It meant they needed someone to help them, an actor who needed a lot of money and who looked similar enough to Jack Kelsall to play the part. Granted, they were in New York with actors living in every third apartment, but they didn't dare expose themselves to the actor, so he would have to be hired in a way that would never lead back to them.

And in a way that could never be traced in any fashion to the execution they were going to commit while he was at the gate.

The second problem was the time. They had less than ten months now. Mary Jo seldom worked under a ticking clock, so this bothered her. Both Jean and Susan said the same thing. Getting in a hurry made for sloppy work and none of them wanted that.

So they split up the tasks that were needed.

Susan would work on how to kill all the drones. With the drones down, that would allow all three of them to move into positions on three sides of the compound. Or at least get away after the shots.

They had located three ideal sniper positions. If the real Jack Kelsall stepped out of his mansion and into that compound open area in front of the main gate at any place, they could drop him.

One nice aspect of their plan was that Kelsall, or as they were starting to call him, the fake-Carson, had a morning exercise routine. He came out of his house every morning without prompting.

Jean's task was to continue to search for any secondary ways in and out of that compound. Once they dropped the drones from the sky, they needed to make sure that the real Kelsall didn't escape before their fake Kelsall arrived at the gate.

They still had to figure out the timing of everything, but they would do that once they reached California.

Mary Jo took on the task of setting up the dummy corporations and overseas accounts that would end up untraceable so that money and instructions could be sent to the actor.

And she was also charged with finding an actor close enough to Kelsall's height and weight and age when Kelsall faked his death and killed his friend.

Three days later Susan had finished her work. The drones would not be a problem.

Jean had found three separate underground tunnels leaving the compound, but all three opened into the California trees close to the sniper positions they had already picked out. So that problem was easily solved as well.

Mary Jo had her task done as well as far as setting up the accounts for all three of them to transfer money into and to hire the actor.

Then she and Susan both went to work on the church finances, trying to figure out ways to hack into their accounts. All three of them had laughingly agreed that if they could take the fake church's money as well as kill their fake leader, it would be a win for everyone involved.

It turned out that draining the church accounts would be a lot easier than any of them had expected. It seemed that over the years the fake Carson had gotten very lax at security in that area.

So finally, Mary Jo felt like they were ready, but for some reason still felt something was wrong.

And that night over dinner, when she said everything felt ready, both Jean and Susan nodded, but not with any enthusiasm.

"I think this is a great plan," Susan said. "And I actually think it will work. But…"

"My problem exactly," Jean said. "But…It feels like we are forgetting one major detail."

Mary Jo looked at Jean, the woman she loved more than anything, and just started laughing.

"It seems," Mary Jo said, "that we have come up with a great plan and there is something about it that bothers all of us. We need to figure out what that is because as old as the three of us are and as long as we have all been doing this, we would be damned foolish to ignore that feeling now."

Jean nodded and then laughed. "First time I've been called old in a very long time."

Mary Jo just smiled at her.

Susan laughed. "Let's not start comparing ages and figure out what piece of this puzzle is missing."

"We take their money," Jean said, holding up one finger. "That will put the church out of business."

"We kill the fake Caron, aka Kelsall," Susan said, holding up two fingers.

"Nothing can be traced to any of us," Jean said, adding a third finger to the tally."

But as they talked Mary Jo knew at once where the problem was.

"We aren't killing Kelsall," Mary Jo said. "As far as the world is concerned, we are killing Carson White, the head of the church. The followers would still all believe that Kelsall will still be returning."

Silence filled the kitchen. Only the faint noise of the city around them painted the background.

Mary Jo knew at once that she had found what had been bothering all of them. Sure, they were killing Kelsall, but only they knew it wasn't Carson White.

And if they killed him like they had planned without anyone knowing the truth, it would set up Carson to be a martyr instead of a scam artist.

None of them wanted that to happen.

They wanted their targets dead.

Nothing more.

CHAPTER THIRTY-SEVEN

JEAN LIKED HOW all three of them were working together. They once again had divided up the tasks they needed to do to round out their plan and expose Kelsall.

Mary Jo finished hiring the actor and got him his instructions and where to pick up his clothes and where to stay when he arrived in San Francisco and so on. And got him his first money.

Mary Jo said he was a nice guy, and it was too bad he was going to have to die for the part.

"Not getting soft on me, are you?" Jean had asked, smiling at Mary Jo. Jean knew for a fact Mary Jo didn't have a soft spot in her body when it came to killing to get to a target. And Jean didn't either.

"Always hate killing nice people to get to bad people," Mary Jo said, shrugging. "But the nature of the job."

"I hate it as well," Jean said. Then she had kissed Mary Jo and they had gone back to work.

Susan was to document every detail about the John Doe body found two days after Kelsall supposedly jumped.

She presented it to Mary Jo and Jean that evening after dinner.

Jean was amazed. Luckily, the coroner had kept the body for two years on ice, as was required by law. And every six months more tests were run on the body, fingerprints taken, and so on, to compare them against missing person's cases around the country.

So there was a major trail of reports and files for that body. Susan seemed to have found them all.

And when the body was finally cremated two years after being found, everything was again well documented, including DNA samples, and the clothing was stored.

Jean was happy to see the DNA samples had been taken, even though DNA was still in its early years back then. That might be the key to discrediting Carson White.

 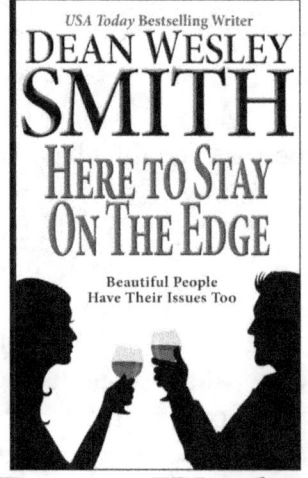 

Some Classic Dean Wesley Smith Stories
Available at your favorite booksellers.

They all agreed that it was worth the effort to get a DNA match, so the next morning Susan left, headed to Washington State. She was going to figure out a way over the next few days to get DNA samples from Carson's still-living mother. Then she would meet Mary Jo and Jean in Sacramento, California.

Mary Jo left also in the morning, heading for California to get them set up out there in a house they had rented, leaving Jean alone in the large condo.

And it shocked Jean how much she instantly didn't like the feeling of being alone. Even after centuries of being alone, living with Mary Jo for a year had changed her.

She didn't want to admit that, but it had.

And she liked the change.

So instead of focusing on the feeling of being alone, she focused on what she needed to do.

She needed to find some explosives in California. She had some escape tunnels to blow up.

CHAPTER THIRTY-EIGHT

MARY JO HAD never been really fond of California, especially the mass of humanity California had become in the last one hundred years. She had fond memories of small towns back over a hundred years ago, but now the entire state felt hot and crowded and angry. Deeply angry.

Mary Jo had a hunch that if she had to spend most of her time on those freeways and stale air, she would be angry as well.

There were a lot more people in New York City, but it felt different.

It took Mary Jo a full day to secure the home she had rented in a nice suburban area of Sacramento. No one would be able to get close to the home without her knowing it, and no one would be able to listen in to any conversation that went on in the home as well.

The place was a standard California ranch-style three-bedroom, with a formal living room, huge modern kitchen that felt cold, and a pool out back with a hot tub attached. The lawn, as it was laughingly called, was a mixture of rock and decorative stone with brush and a few palm trees. Nothing to water, that was for sure. There were more green plants in their condo in New York City than this home had around it.

And it was so warm outside, and the air so full of smog, Mary Jo doubted that she and Jean would even use the hot tub.

They didn't plan on being here for more than a month, but the landlord didn't know that. Mary Jo had paid a hefty deposit and first and last on a year's lease. The name she had used could never actually be traced to her when the property owner and management company came looking long after they were gone.

Susan had rented a condo in a nice area near the river, and then Jean had rented another house within a mile of the church compound, but none of them would sleep there, and when in the house would always wear gloves with fake fingerprints. They would use that place for staging and nothing more.

They planned on blowing up the house when finished to erase most evidence of their presence there, but better to be safe than sorry with leaving traces and fingerprints.

Mary Jo had rented a tan Jeep SUV for the month. The entire time on the plane and renting the car and talking with the real estate agent, Mary Jo had worn a light-blonde wig, a fake nose that was wider and flatter, and green contacts under large-rimmed glasses.

Jean would be in disguise as well any time the two of them moved outside in any fashion. Their plan was that none of them would ever be seen by anyone. But just in case that part of the plan went wrong, they took no chances.

Mary Jo had unpacked her few things in the master bedroom closet, laughing at how little room her clothes took up in the huge space. Then she wandered back into the massive kitchen and just stood there, looking around.

Damn, she wanted to just call Jean, but she didn't. They needed to stick to plan, but at the moment Mary Jo didn't much like the plan of her being alone in this tomb of a house without Jean.

Finally, she clicked on the alarms she had set and headed into the massive three-car garage where her rental Jeep sat looking sort of small and alone.

"We need some dinner and to stock the fridge," Mary Jo said out loud. Her voice echoed and she laughed. "And maybe even buy a few plates as well."

She had work to do over the next three days until Jean arrived. That was what she would focus on.

For thousands of years, her work had been enough for her. It would be enough for three days as well.

But that didn't stop her wanting Jean beside her in the car. Not one bit.

CHAPTER THIRTY-NINE

JEAN WAS REALLY happy to see Mary Jo waiting for her in the airport. Of course, Mary Jo as a blonde with glasses and a large nose didn't look like Mary Jo, but Jean would have known her anywhere.

Jean had on a brown wig, brown contacts, and some fake eyebrows that made them look thick and bushy over her thin glasses.

Mary Jo hugged her and Jean was startled how wonderful it felt. Even better than she had been thinking it would feel. The two of them just fit together in so many ways.

"I've missed you," Mary Jo said as they turned and headed for the parking area.

"I missed you as well," Jean said. "More than I want to admit."

Mary Jo smiled. "I know that feeling."

An hour later they were seated at the counter in the massive kitchen of the house Mary Jo had rented. The place was decorated in white and black and metal handles and had about as much warmth as a steel mill. Jean had hated it the moment Mary Jo had let her in the door from the garage.

Mary Jo had agreed. "This place feels more like a fancy prison cell than a home."

"Imagine the couples who think this is their style," Jean said, looking around. "I don't want to think about what their relationship would really be like?"

"Sterile and by the numbers," Mary Jo had said, shuddering.

Mary Jo had gotten them both glasses of iced tea.

"So are we about set?" Mary Jo asked. "I've got ready everything we need here. And our fake Jack Kelsall has arrived and is waiting for word while spending vast amounts of money drinking and eating as he was told to do, all on the expense account."

"My parts of the plan are in place," Jean said, smiling.

At that very moment Mary Jo's phone beeped. Mary Jo glanced at it, then smiled.

"Susan has turned into the main subdivision street and will be here in one minute."

"Tracking?" Jean asked.

"Tracking," Mary Jo said. "I'll get her a glass of iced tea, you want to go into the garage and open a door for her?"

"Gladly," Jean said, heading out into what felt more like an empty sports facility than a garage. In New York entire families could live comfortably in smaller spaces.

As the automatic door opened onto the heat of the day and the white, filtered sunlight, a blue compact appeared around a corner. Within thirty seconds, the blue car was in the garage and the garage door was closing.

Susan climbed out, her black hair now turned silver and her nose upturned and dark-rimmed glasses. She also had grown a pair of boobs somewhere along the way. She looked fifteen years older than she had in New York.

"Mary Jo's pouring you a glass of iced tea," Jean said as Susan got her small bag from the back of the car. "Any success?"

Susan smiled, showing some false caps on her teeth that yellowed them some. "Oh, wonderful success. Wait until you see it all."

Jean felt that slight surge of excitement she always felt when about ready to start a job. Preparation was almost finished.

At some point very soon they would make the go or no-go decision.

And that would signal the start of the first time she had worked with two other assassins. Until meeting Mary Jo, she would have never thought working with just one other would be possible.

Jean just hoped this worked as planned.

But of course, she always felt that way before starting a job.

Always.

PART NINE
Execution

CHAPTER FORTY

THE DARK NIGHT surrounded Mary Jo like a welcoming blanket. The night air was still warm and the dryness of the forest underbrush made almost any movement a possible noisy step.

She had on night vision goggles and could see fairly clearly from the light gathered in from what few stars got through the smog and haze that seemed to perpetually cover this area of the state. It wasn't a damp haze, either, but felt like a dry smoke instead.

Mary Jo settled into a crouch, studying her watch for the exact right moment to move. The drones that guarded the area around the church compound were automatic and set on an exact schedule. Mary Jo could hear the background buzzing of all of them in the area, but one drone noise seemed to get louder for a moment as she stayed very still.

Within seconds, the drone moved past her. There was no chance it could see her since she was dressed in complete black and the drones did not carry any form of heat sensor. As long as she didn't move when it passed overhead, it wouldn't see her.

That alone was a fatal flaw in an otherwise pretty solid drone defense of the area outside the church walls. That flaw had allowed them to not bring down the drones until the actual attack. Much better timing.

She gave the drone a moment to get past her location and then kept moving, making no sound at all as she moved along the dry ground cover.

In another thirty seconds she was at the hidden exit of the escape tunnel from the church. At one point, after finding the location of the escape tunnels, they had considered just going into the church that way, but all of them agreed there were just too many unknowns inside.

And all three of them had survived for centuries not allowing unknowns to be a part of any plan.

Mary Jo hated unknowns. At the moment, she felt that there were no unknowns at all in this plan.

It had been three days since Susan and Jean had joined her again here in California. And what Susan had found to prove that Jack Kelsall really was imitating Carson White was stunning.

She not only had DNA evidence that the John Doe body was Carson, but she had found and talked with three of the fake Carson's former boyfriends.

Jilted boyfriends, it seems. And they had been more than willing to give her dirt on some personal stuff about the fake Carson. Things like he wasn't a real blond but instead just dyed his hair and wore colored contacts.

The three of them had put all the information together in very clean packets, with names, dates, data, and evidence. Then yesterday they had sent out the packets to every jurisdiction that might have standing in the case of fraud and murder.

Turns out for the fraud, that was a lot of jurisdictions. The fake church had really spread out.

And at the same time they had sent out the same information to every major news source in California and Nevada.

It was clear in the packets of information how it would be possible to back up the fact that Jack Kelsall had killed Carson White. They sent the videos of the fall, pointing out some things in the videos not seen before, such as the falling body's hair color. Modern film forensics could do wonders with older recordings.

They also detailed in the information how Kelsall as fake Carson had been bilking people out of millions for over twenty years with phony promises.

And just for good measure, they had tossed in how he had been cheating the government on the taxes as well since the church was a scam.

Jack Kelsall, aka fake Carson White, was set up for a huge fall.

So this afternoon, right before they left the suburban house for the last time, they drained all of the fake Carson White's personal millions as well as every dime the fake church had.

Mary Jo had loved watching Susan and Jean do that.

And they made it all look as if the fake Carson had moved the money offshore and was about to flee because he was being exposed.

The three of them were now many, many millions richer each. The money didn't matter to them, but for Mary Jo it sure felt right to do.

Again, the sound of an approaching drone over her head made her crouch and study her watch.

Exactly on time.

Mary Jo waited until a drone passed overhead, then carefully opened the escape hatch just enough to not trigger any alarms.

Moving slowly, she pulled a long black package from her backpack and slid it inside the hatch.

She then closed the escape hatch carefully.

At that moment she knew that Jean and Susan were doing exactly the same thing at the other two hatches.

Mary Jo moved slowly back away from the hatch until she was at a safe distance, then set the trigger to the explosive package. The plan was to set all three off at once. But now the package would explode if anyone got near it while trying to use the escape hatch.

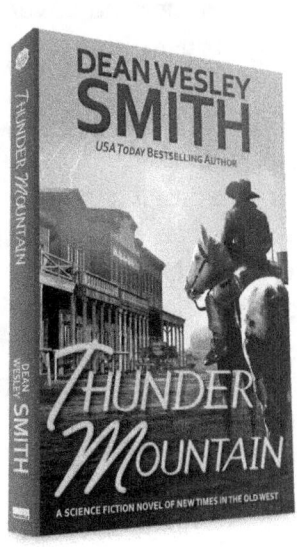

Mary Jo just hoped the fake Carson didn't try to leave tonight through any of the tunnels. There would hardly be enough left of him to do a DNA test on if he did.

Again Mary Jo crouched and kept completely still until a drone passed overhead, then silently she moved back into the forest.

It was almost time.

CHAPTER FORTY-ONE

JEAN EASED HERSELF into position between two small trees and under some brush. She didn't need her night vision anymore because the lights of the compound gave her more than enough light to see.

She was on a ridge above the compound and could see most of the buildings and the open area and the stone guard building beside the front gate.

She had her custom-made sniper rifle set up in front of her and covered slightly in some lose brush. It was a pure black color and deadly.

The drones were going to drop in another fifteen minutes, but until then, she needed to stay completely hidden and still.

Since there had been no explosion or alarm, she knew that both Susan and Mary Jo were also now in positions, rifles ready.

Jean had kissed Mary Jo goodbye as they had parted from their staging house. They wouldn't see each other for almost a week as they made their way back to New York, changing identities and looks a few times along the way.

They all had to make sure that there was no chance that what happened here could ever be traced back to any of them in any fashion. Being completely careful like that had kept her alive and working and out of prison for a couple thousand years now. She didn't plan on changing that status any time soon.

And she loved how both Mary Jo and Susan were equally as careful. The three of them worked well as a team, of that there was no doubt. This entire plan would have never worked without all three of them, actually.

Jean settled in and used the scope on her rifle to study the compound below her. It looked a little like a California subdivision, with houses on both sides of a large common park area. And a large mansion set back up the hill.

Everything was clean, almost too clean, and well-landscaped. All the green grass and lush trees showed that this church didn't believe in any water shortage.

Every morning at sunrise, Carson had a regular schedule. He came out of his mansion and led an exercise routine in the park area near the front entrance. She and Mary Jo and Susan were betting Carson would do that again today.

The evening news had been full of reports about the church after the packages of proof that it was a scam reached the news outlets. It hadn't taken some of them long to collaborate the proof and get it on the air. So Jean had no doubt that the fake Carson knew he needed to pretend everything was all right.

It was when the fake Carson was to do his exercise that the actor they had hired was due to arrive. He would pull up and say he was Jack Kelsall and needed to talk to his partner, Carson White.

Either the normal routine or the fake Jack Kelsall showing up would be enough to bring the real Kelsall, aka Carson White, out of his mansion.

The backup plan if either of those things didn't happen was to stay in place and kill the real Kelsall when the police came and arrested him.

To Jean that third backup felt very risky, but they all had their routes to get away carefully planned. It would work, just not her favorite option by a long ways.

Jean felt the watch on her wrist tingle slightly against her skin.

Two minutes until the fake Carson appeared and walked down to the exercise area.

Jean took a deep breath and made herself focus forward.

It was time.

Above her a drone went past without seeing her.

And from her position, far down the valley, she could see the car with the actor playing the part of Jack Kelsall coming up the valley.

Everything was in motion.

Perfect so far.

CHAPTER FORTY-TWO

MARY JO LAY perfectly still as a drone moved over her head and past her position. She lay covered in brush, facing the church compound below her. She was on the left of the compound main gate, Jean was on the right.

Susan had taken a spot higher on the hill toward the back of the compound.

Mary Jo had on a black suit, a black face mask with only her eyes exposed, black thin gloves and her rifle was pure black.

She felt calm and almost relaxed.

She was ready.

From down the valley she could see the actor's car approaching the compound.

Dozens of the faithful, all in bright exercise clothes, were stretching and chatting on the large lawn area to the right of the main gate, waiting for their leader. Mary Jo wondered how many of them had seen the morning news so far.

The church they believed in, the man they believed in, was getting torn apart in the press. Mary Jo had no doubt the police wouldn't be far behind. They police didn't dare wait too long since they had clear evidence that the fake Carson was really Jack Kelsall who had killed the real Carson White and actually filmed his body going off the bridge.

Mary Jo hoped that the real Jack Kelsall would actually be dead by the time the police arrived.

The sun was just about to hit the tops of the Sierras behind the compound when the front door to the mansion opened and the fake Carson White stepped out.

Mary Jo sighted in on him. She could see him look around and smile as if nothing at all was wrong in the world. Then he started down his front walk toward the sidewalk that would take him down the hill to the park and his followers.

He seemed totally unconcerned that his entire world had exploded in the press and all his money had vanished into his pretend accounts and then vanished from there.

Could the guy not even listen to the news? Was it possible he kept himself and his followers that shut off from the world inside these walls?

And was it possible none of his followers checked the bank accounts every morning?

From the smile on the guy's face, it sure seemed that way.

Mary Jo was stunned that someone this complacent had gotten away with so much for so long.

The fake Carson was about halfway down the hill to the park, strolling along easily when the fake Jack Kelsall stopped his car just down from the gate and got out and walked toward the gate.

The timing was perfect. Just perfect.

The gate was two huge iron gates with a stone guardhouse built into one of the walls to the right.

Mary Jo kept her gun trained on their target, but watched the event at the gate play out.

In ten seconds after the actor reached the gate, one of the guards came out of the gatehouse building and ran at a sprint up the hill toward the fake Carson.

The fake Carson had been about to turn to join his followers in the park when the guard reached him and indicated he come to the guardhouse.

The remaining three guards at the front gate had let the fake Kelsall stand just inside the gate and closed it again behind him.

So now, as they had planned, the fake Kelsall was facing the fake Carson as he came down the hill.

Mary Jo was thrilled that this was working exactly as planned. It was playing out as they imagined it would.

As the fake Carson got within ten steps of the fake Jack Kelsall, Jack raised his hand and Carson stopped.

Perfect.

The young actor was playing his lines perfectly.

Mary Jo, Susan, and Jean all now had clean shots of everyone participating.

About ten of the followers and the four armed-guards all stood staring at what was happening in front of them, but all kept their distance.

Mary Jo and Jean and Susan knew the exact words the young actor was speaking. Exactly.

Mary Jo watched carefully, the rifle centered on the chest of the fake Carson.

The actor was asking Carson why he had duped so many people, why he had pretended to be someone he wasn't.

Carson shook his head.

At that moment, the actor pounded his chest as he was supposed to do in this part of his speech.

Mary Jo fired.

She was just a fraction of a second behind either Susan or Jean.

Carson's chest had exploded when Mary Jo's shot got there and blew it apart even more. A high-velocity rifle shot using hollow-point ammunition could do that to a body. Small entrance wound, huge exist hole.

And from the looks of it, another bullet tore into the fake Carson at the same moment Mary Jo's shot had hit him.

It was lucky the three shots hadn't cut the guy in half. But there was no doubt he was dead.

Mary Jo turned her rifle on the startled actor and shot him before the fake Carson's body hit the ground.

"Sorry kid," Mary Jo said. "But your last part was played to award-winning levels."

Jean and Susan picked off two of the guards at the same time.

Mary Jo went to the guard near one wall and dropped him as Jean and Susan dropped the other two guards at the front gate.

Then a massive explosion echoed over the valley as Jean blew up the three bombs in the escape tunnels.

At that moment Susan shut down all the drones and one fell in the brush close to where Mary Jo was. And Mary Jo knew that Susan also sent a signal back to the computers controlling the drones that she hoped would destroy the computers, but it actually didn't matter if that worked or not.

A moment later Mary Jo took out another guard coming out of one building and Jean and Susan dropped two other guards who had appeared near the parking area.

Mary Jo let herself take a moment to study the scene below. The real Jack Kelsall, who had been hiding as Carson White, lay dead in a pool of his own blood on the driveway leading into his fake-church compound.

The actor playing Jack Kelsall sprawled near him.

All the people who had been waiting to exercise with their church leader were now getting their exercise running at full speed for cover.

Susan had set up automatic calls to the local police and they would be coming up the road shortly.

The job was done.

The target was eliminated.

It was time to go.

Mary Jo eased back away from the ridge, made sure she had left nothing where she had been. Not only did she have on the black suit, but she also wore man's boots too large for her feet.

Jean and Susan had done the same, so it would be assumed that three men of medium height and size had done this, not three small, cute women.

Mary Jo picked her way down the ridgeline, moving quickly, but not recklessly.

Twenty minutes later she dug out a small blue backpack from a pile of brush. The pack had a change of clothes in it.

Standing under a grove of dry trees, she changed out of the boots and into tennis shoes, out of the black suit and into white shorts and a low-cut blouse. She took off the black gloves, but left on thin gloves with fake fingerprints.

She pulled off the black stocking cap that had covered her hair and put on a blonde wig.

She used a wipe to take off the black from her face that the mask didn't cover and put everything in the backpack.

She took out a bottle of water, took a drink and put the bottle back. That one simple drink of water tasted wonderful.

Then she quickly took the rifle apart and put it in the backpack as well.

Within two minutes she was walking down the trail like a college girl out for a morning hike.

In the next valley over she could hear police sirens echoing through the morning air.

She had a pretty good hike over another ridgeline away from the compound to a small rental car she had parked there at a trailhead.

But by nine in the morning she would be in Nevada and headed south toward Las Vegas.

She liked Las Vegas. She might spend time there before heading for New York.

But she had a hunch it wouldn't be long. She was already missing Jean.

And their hot tub.

CHAPTER FORTY-THREE

TWENTY-FOUR HOURS after the attack on the church compound, Jean sat eating breakfast at a wonderful diner just outside of Spokane, Washington. The place had a 1950s feel and smelled of rich coffee and cinnamon rolls.

It had taken her about twenty minutes to get off the ridgeline above the church compound and to where she had stashed a backpack full of clothes.

Hiding in deep brush to make sure no one flying overhead would see her, she had changed clothes, taken her rifle apart, and had everything in the pack. Twenty minutes after stopping she was headed up a trail and over yet another ridgeline away from the compound.

Two hours later she reached a Cadillac she had parked there and headed back down the hill and into Sacramento.

From there, without stopping, she had gotten on I-5 and headed north toward Oregon, setting the cruise control and letting the air-conditioning keep her comfortable in the warming morning.

She had stopped for a late breakfast in Redding and a late lunch in Eugene.

Dinner had been in a fast-food place south of Olympia.

Now, after driving most of the night, stopping only to rest and catch a few naps and drop parts of her rifle in a river, she was having a wonderful and leisurely breakfast while watching the news on a television behind the diner's counter.

It had been just over twenty-four hours.

It seemed that the story about deaths at a cult church in California led most of the news programs and there were worries it was terrorist in nature.

But saner voices on the news were saying it was revenge, clearly, for Jack Kelsall creating a false church and duping so many millions of people.

The police had no suspects at all. And no one mentioned that all the church money had vanished.

After she finished her breakfast, Jean turned away from the news and just sat thinking while she sipped a cup of coffee. Mary Jo would be in Vegas by now and Jean wished she was there with her.

And Susan had headed south to LA and then east toward Phoenix. No telling where she would be, but she had seemed excited about going in that direction for some reason.

Jean had to admit that she had really loved working with Mary Jo and Susan on this target. And having the three of them made the end of this job so much better than it would have been.

Susan had even offered to split her final payment with them, since before they had joined she hadn't even been able to find Kelsall, let alone expose and kill him.

But both Jean and Mary Jo had turned her down. Neither of them needed the money in the slightest. Money was just how they kept score, how a life was valued in their business.

And with the fake Carson money and the church money, Jean figured they were each about sixty million richer anyway. She doubted she would ever get around to counting it.

Now, if the final part of the plan held, Jean would meet Mary Jo in their condo in New York at some point in the next week.

Susan had no plans. She had said she would see them when she saw them.

Jean understood that. Until falling in love with Mary Jo, Jean could have never imagined working with another assassin, let alone looking forward to going back to be with one.

But at the same time, it wouldn't surprise Jean in the slightest if Mary Jo never came back. She had been independent for as long, if not longer than Jean had. Vanishing now would be an easy way to just call the relationship off.

But Jean knew, without a doubt, she would be in that condo in New York hoping that Mary Jo showed up. And she would live there for a time, even if Mary Jo decided to not show up.

Jean wouldn't blame Mary Jo if she didn't return.

But Jean would really, really miss her.

CHAPTER FORTY-FOUR

MARY JO SAT at a half-filled bar in the Bellagio Hotel and Casino and sipped a vodka orange juice. She had spent the afternoon buying new clothes and was now about as dressed up as she ever got. For some reason she had felt she wanted to put on a short dress, new jewelry, and new shoes.

All expensive.

Now, from a table about thirty feet away, two men in suits, clearly dressed down from their day job normal, were watching her as she sat at the bar, showing more leg than she probably needed to. Likely they thought she was an expensive lady of the evening and were wondering if they could afford her.

Wouldn't they be surprised if they knew she was a cold killer?

She kind of smiled at that and turned away from being able to see the men, instead sort of staring at herself in the mirror behind the bar as she sipped on her drink.

She wasn't sure why she wanted to get dressed up, but after a job well done, it seemed appropriate to treat herself to a good drink and a nice lobster dinner. She had even put on make-up and got her hair trimmed and styled a little.

She actually did look expensive.

After most jobs she had done something similar to this. New clothes, great drinks, and an expensive dinner in a form of celebration.

But for some reason this time it didn't feel right.

Jean belonged here with her.

They were planning on meeting back at the condo in New York in a few days, but Mary Jo wasn't sure Jean would return.

Being an assassin for so long had made Jean into a loner, just as Mary Jo was a loner. Mary Jo had always enjoyed the time alone, never really thought about being any other way.

But that was before Jean.

She finished the last of her vodka orange juice and pushed the change from her drink forward as a sign it was a tip for the bartender.

Then, with a glance at the two men staring at her from a side table, she headed out into the crowded and noisy walkways of the casino.

She didn't feel like partying alone tonight. She hadn't done the job alone, she needed to party with Jean.

Five minutes later she was in her suite and had changed out of her new dress and shoes and put on comfortable traveling clothes of jeans, a sports bra, a silk blouse, and new tennis shoes.

Twenty minutes later she had her new clothes packed into a carry-on bag and headed to the airport. That morning she had sold her car at a local used car lot after cleaning it completely.

As she often did, she had booked and paid for five first-class tickets to New York, one for each evening she had planned to be in Las Vegas. She hated feeling trapped in a city because of

booked flights, so about twenty years ago she had started doing that.

She had thought she might stay at least two or three days in Vegas, but she had gone ahead and booked the tickets for all five possible days because she figured she didn't know when she would want to leave.

She sort of laughed at herself that she hadn't lasted a day relaxing without Jean.

Not one single day.

Wow, she really was in love.

And she didn't mind that at all.

CHAPTER FORTY-FIVE

JEAN GOT A good night's sleep in a wonderful suite hotel just outside of Missoula, Montana. Then the next day she had spent buying some new comfortable clothes and donating the last of the clothing she had worn in California to different charities around the town.

Then she donated her car to a charity after making sure it was rubbed clean completely of any fingerprints or trace she had been in it. She signed over the title under one of her fake names.

From there, she headed to the airport.

Five hours later she was in a cab headed into Denver.

She had no idea why she had decided to go to Denver. It just seemed logical and as the cab pulled into the hotel she had booked, she just flat changed her mind.

She didn't want to be here. She wanted to be in New York, in her and Mary Jo's condo.

So she had the cab driver wait and she went in and cancelled her reservation, then had the cab take her back to the airport. The poor driver was smiling the entire way, thinking he had managed to get the best client ever.

By paying a little extra and flirting with a woman at the counter, Jean managed to get on a late flight to New York through Chicago.

By three in the morning New York time, the cab dropped her off in front of the condo.

The air was muggy and the sounds of the city wrapped around her like a welcome hug. Damn she loved this city. She felt like she was home.

She stared up at the condo, but could see no lights in the windows, so she put her bag over her shoulder and turned and headed up the sidewalk to a deli. She was hungry and she knew they had left nothing to eat in the condo.

On top of that, she needed to buy some fresh orange juice. She planned on having a drink tonight and soaking in the hot tub. And then getting a long, long night's sleep in her and Mary Jo's bed.

Twenty minutes later, her travel bag over one shoulder and a sack of groceries in both hands, she was one block from the condo when she saw a cab pull up.

Jean kept walking, smiling, as the most beautiful woman in the entire world climbed out of the cab with a light travel bag and stood on the sidewalk staring upward.

Jean was within twenty steps of Mary Jo when she turned and looked at her and broke into a huge smile.

"Didn't want to go up there alone," Mary Jo said, coming to Jean and stepping into her arms as Jean put the groceries on the sidewalk.

For Jean, it was the best hug she had felt in a very, very long time.

Then after a very long kiss, Jean smiled at the woman she loved and indicated the groceries. "I had to get some orange juice and something to eat."

"A woman after my own heart," Mary Jo said, smiling.

"I was hoping I already had it," Jean said.

"Oh, you do," Mary Jo said. "You really do."

~

Coming Next Issue in *Smith's Monthly*

#1...October 2013

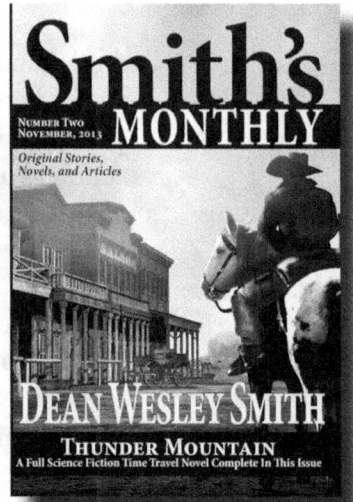

#2...November 2013

#3...December 2013

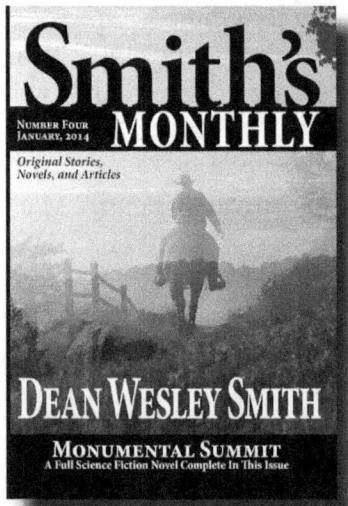

#4...January 2014

#5...February 2014

#6...March 2014

#7...April 2014

#8...May 2014

#9...June 2014

#10...July 2014

#11...August 2014

#12...September 2014

#13...October 2014

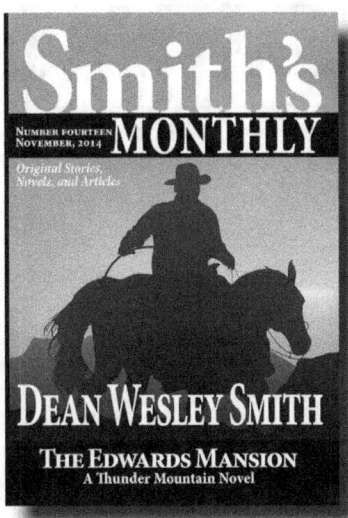

#14...November 2014

#15...December 2014

#16...January 2015

#17...February 2015

#18...March 2015

#19...April 2015

#20...May 2015

#21...June 2015

#22...July 2015

#23...August 2015

#24...September 2015

#25...October 2015

#26...November 2015

#27...December 2015

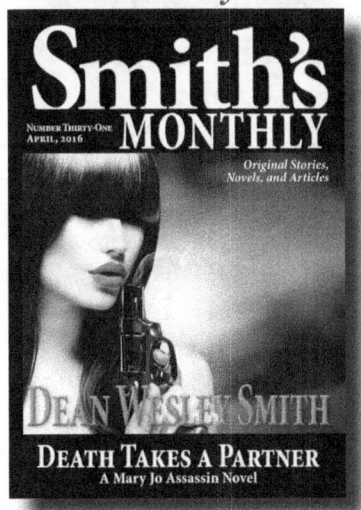

Thank You!!

I would like to thank the following wonderful people who support my blog and my work through Patreon. Your support is very important to me. Thanks!

Betsy Wilcox
Irette Y. Patterson
Kathryn Rooney
Wendy Lee Maddox
Jamie Curierre
Chris Cousino
Jane Lawson
Shantnu Tiwari
Miguel Angel Alonso Pulido
Nancy Hendrickson
Ryan M. Williams
Jacob Proffitt
Marian Goldeen
Gary Speer
Megan Bryce
Michelle Tatam
Ann Tucker
Kari Wolfe
Albert Lemke
Stacey Larson
Diane Darcy
Krystle Jones
Kari Gallagher
T. Thorn Coyle
Tasha Turner Lennhoff

Erick Lindman
Christopher Ridge
Terry Mixon
James Husun
Sherman Cox
Chong Go
Maria Grace
Grondpom
Fen
Robin Brande
J.R. Murdock
Kathleen McClure
Gunnar Gunderson
F.I. Goldhaber
Mary Jo Rabe
John Kilgallon
Dave Hendrickson
Jabberwocky
Eric Goebelbecker
Marsha Kessler
Scott Gordon
Martyn Folkes
John
Cj Lehi
Brenda Smith

www.ingramcontent.com/pod-product-compliance
Lightning Source LLC
Chambersburg PA
CBHW081152170626
46813CB00009B/3171